Eva

The sight of Samantha Corley placing tiny baby socks and cuddly sleepers in the drawer made his stomach feel funny.

This scene felt way too domestic and cozy to suit him. Sam was actually humming. Humming, for God's sake.

He lowered his head, trying to ignore this soft, feminine side of her. Sam had always been a tomboy. And right now, she was scaring the hell out of him because he was beginning to actually like being with her.

No, he wouldn't let this get personal. He'd protect her and the child until they found out the truth.

Then Sam could do whatever she wanted, and he'd move on with his plans to leave town.

RITA HERRON

PEEK-A-BOO PROTECTOR

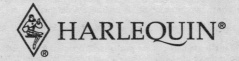

HARLEQUIN®

TORONTO • NEW YORK • LONDON
AMSTERDAM • PARIS • SYDNEY • HAMBURG
STOCKHOLM • ATHENS • TOKYO • MILAN • MADRID
PRAGUE • WARSAW • BUDAPEST • AUCKLAND

To Allison & Denise—
two great editors who sparked this idea!

Recycling programs
for this product may
not exist in your area.

ISBN-13: 978-0-373-69426-6

PEEK-A-BOO PROTECTOR

ABOUT THE AUTHOR

Award-winning author Rita Herron wrote her first book when she was twelve, but didn't think real people grew up to be writers. Now she writes so she doesn't have to get a *real* job. A former kindergarten teacher and workshop leader, she traded storytelling to kids for romance, and writes romantic comedies and romantic suspense. She lives in Georgia with her own romance hero and three kids. She loves to hear from readers so please write her at P.O. Box 921225, Norcross, GA 30092-1225, or visit her Web site at www.ritaherron.com.

Books by Rita Herron

HARLEQUIN INTRIGUE

*Nighthawk Island
**Guardian Angel Investigations

CAST OF CHARACTERS

Police Chief John Wise—He'll do anything to protect Samantha Corley and the baby left on her doorstep.

Samantha Corley—She needs John's protection for her and the baby, but she can't lose her heart to the man.

Honey Dawson—She left her baby daughter at Samantha's house. Is Honey dead or alive?

Dwayne Hicks—Honey's high school boyfriend. Did he find out she'd come back to town and kill her for dumping him?

Sally Rae Hicks—Did Dwayne's wife kill Honey because she thought Honey wanted to reunite with Dwayne?

Judge Teddy Wexler—He thinks Honey's twins are his. Would he kill Honey to get the twins back?

Portia Wexler—She claims she'll help Teddy raise the twins as part of their family.

Teddy Wexler Junior—He doesn't mind his father's affairs, but how far would he go to keep from sharing his inheritance with one of his father's whores or her bastard brats?

Tiffany Maylor—Honey's rival for the cheerleading spot with the Dallas Cowboys—would she hurt Honey to ensure she wins that spot?

Jimmy Bartow—The bailiff is in love with Honey. Would he kill her out of spite for leaving him for the judge?

Neil Kinney—Honey's stalker.

Reed Tanner—Another one of Honey's lovers. He claims he's looking for her, but he obviously has secrets and doesn't trust the cops.

Prologue

Leaving her baby was the hardest thing Honey Dawson had ever done.

But someone was trying to kill her, and she had to run. Had to in order to keep her babies safe.

She swiped at the tears trickling down her face and gulped back a sob. Beside her, her baby girl cooed up at her so innocently that her heart wrenched.

"I'm not a deserter, Emmie," she said earnestly as her baby boy's face taunted her. "I'll go back and get your brother and we'll all be together again one day."

She wouldn't be like her own mother who'd left her on the doorstep of the local orphanage with nothing but a diaper and an empty locket. She hadn't even put a picture inside. Hadn't even given her a name.

The caretakers had called her Honey because of her golden hair, and Dawson for the county she was left in. It was downright pitiful.

The reason she'd taken such good care to choose special names for her twins. "When I get us out of this mess, we'll be a family, I promise." Another sob escaped her. "I may have messed up but I swear on my mama's necklace—" she stroked the pendant she always wore, one that now held her twins' pictures "—I swear that I'll be a good mama."

Butterville, the small town where she'd grown up, loomed ahead with its welcoming arms, and she crossed the county line and veered the car toward Samantha Corley's house. Sam was the only real friend Honey had ever known.

Men adored Honey, but girls didn't take much to her.

Of course, lately she'd pissed off both sexes. Now one of them wanted her dead.

Trouble was, she wasn't even sure who....

No, she wasn't going to die. She had babies to live for now, and Honey would not let anyone stop her from raising them. Sam would help. Sam always knew what to do.

Her foster sister lived on the side of the mountain in a little cabin that had been there for decades. So like Sam to still be here. She probably hadn't changed a stick of furniture or her hairstyle, for that matter.

Honey hadn't been able to get away fast enough. She'd wanted to follow her dreams. Now the town felt like she was coming home, and her only dream was to take care of the twins.

Honey checked over her shoulder for the umpteenth time, but she didn't spot anyone following her. Thank God. She'd finally lost the son of a bitch who'd followed her across the country.

She slowed the vehicle, her heart fluttering as the car lights flickered off the porch swing where she and Sam had shared lazy afternoons drinking sweet tea, dreaming about their futures and trading secrets.

But Sam's house looked dark as Hades, and she

didn't see a car anywhere nearby, so she parked and cut the lights. Emmie had fallen asleep, so she left her in the car long enough to check the front door. It was locked. She searched the flowerpot where Sam usually kept a key. Darn it, it was gone.

Not to worry though. A locked door never kept Honey Dawson out.

She removed a hairpin and jimmied the door open in five seconds flat. The night shadows seemed ominous, the whistle of the wind as eerie as the mountain lion's howl. She scanned the trees surrounding the house and shivered. Someone could be hiding in those woods, ready to pounce.

No, she was safe. Finally. Sam would take care of her. Help her figure out what to do. Then they'd get her little boy back.

She rushed back to the car, grabbed the diaper bag and then the infant carrier and car seat base. "I love you, kitten," she purred. Smiling at her daughter, she juggled the carrier and bag up the steps, shut the door and went straight to the kitchen to heat a bottle. The sweet scent of chocolate-chip cookies warmed the air and memories suffused her.

But a noise startled her. The wind? Leaves crunching? A stray dog scrounging in the garbage for food?

Boards creaked as if someone was climbing the back steps.

Trembling, she grabbed the baby and diaper bag and rushed up the staircase to Sam's room. Determined to protect Emmie, she opened the closet door, set the baby and bag inside then pulled the door closed.

Fisting her hands by her side to defend herself, she tiptoed down the stairs, then heard a noise in the kitchen and ran to the back door to make sure it was locked. But it stood open, a gust of cold fall air swirling through the room blowing dry leaves into the entryway.

Suddenly someone grabbed her from behind and pressed a knife to her throat. She kicked and screamed, clawing for something to use as a weapon. She grabbed a glass from the counter, but he knocked it from her hand, and it fell onto the floor and shattered. Shouting an obscenity, he tightened his grip and dragged her toward the door. They knocked a chair over as they struggled, then the blade pierced her skin, and warm blood oozed down her neck.

"Where's the snotty brat?" he growled.

"Somewhere far from here," she cried, "someplace safe."

He jabbed the knife deeper, piercing her shoulder blade. "Tell me or I'll kill you."

Honey had to get him out of the house. "Just don't hurt me. I'll take you to her."

A car engine rumbled in the graveled drive. Her attacker cursed and dragged her out the back door. She bit and kicked at him, aiming her foot toward his groin, but he slapped her so hard her ears rang and the world swirled blindly.

Still she tried to scream, but the sound died as he dragged her into the woods to kill her.

Chapter One

"You'll be sorry you messed with me."

Leonard Cultrain's angry words echoed through Samantha Corley's head as she drove up the winding graveled drive to her cabin. His mother, Lou Lou, one of the most bitter, crotchety old ladies she'd ever known, had insisted that her son was innocent of murdering his wife, that he never should have been arrested in the first place.

But everyone in town knew Leonard was out of jail on a technicality, and the residents were on edge.

Gravel spewed behind her as she pressed the accelerator and screeched up her driveway. Normally she wasn't skittish, and could hold her own, but she'd feel a hell of a lot better once she was inside her house with her shotgun by her side.

Usually Sam liked living out here alone in the wilderness, but today the isolation felt eerie.

The thick dense trees rocked with the wind, the branches dipping like big hands trying to reach her, hands like Leonard's.

Hands that could choke her just like he'd choked his wife.

Stop it; you're just being paranoid. You're home now.

But her headlights flickered across the lawn as she braked, and she spotted a strange car parked in front of her house.

An uneasy feeling rippled up her spine. Had Leonard come to make good on his threat?

No, this wasn't Leonard's old car.

The license plate was from Fulton County, the Atlanta area. She didn't know anyone from Atlanta.

Maybe she should call the local police. Chief John Wise's strong masculine face flashed in her mind, and for a brief moment, she wished that he was here. That he'd take charge and make sure she was safe.

But she couldn't depend on a man. She'd learned that a long damn time ago. Besides, John would only fuss at her for going out to Leonard's. He thought she was foolish to go up against bullies like him.

The infuriating man was like most others she knew. They wanted a dainty little female, one they could protect—and control.

Sam was none of those things. In foster care, she'd learned to do the protecting and to stand up for herself.

Besides, tangling with the tall, dark brooding cop rattled her every time—and made her want things she couldn't have. Like a man in her life....

No, she'd check this out for herself. Maybe she simply had a visitor.

Yeah, right. Sam didn't have a lot of friends. Acquaintances, yes, but no one she shared her secrets with. No one to sleep over.

Not since Honey had left.

Clenching her cell phone in one hand, she grabbed the baseball bat she kept with her from the backseat floorboard and climbed out.

Slowly she moved up the porch steps, glancing at the windows and searching for movement inside the house, listening for sounds of an intruder. If a car was here, someone had to be around. But where?

Her senses sprang to alert at the top of the steps. The front door had been jimmied. She held her breath and inched forward, then touched the doorknob. It felt icy against her finger, then the door swung open with a screech.

She exhaled shakily. Inside, the house was dark, the smell of fear palpable. But another scent drifted to her. A man's cologne. Heavy. Cheap. Too strong.

She hesitated and moved behind the door. She'd be a fool to go inside. She had to call for help.

But a baby's cry pierced the air. A *baby?* God, what if the child was hurt? If the parent was here for her help?

It was a small town. Everyone knew what she did for a living, that she was a children's advocate, a guardian ad litem, and sometimes they needed her help.

Her heart stuttered in her chest. If the child was in danger, she couldn't wait.

Still she had to be cautious. She inched into the entryway, but froze at the sight of blood in the kitchen.

Someone was hurt.

Trembling, she slipped into the corner behind the door and punched 9-1-1, then whispered that she had an intruder.

"We'll get someone there ASAP," the dispatch officer said. "Stay on the line."

But the baby wailed again, and she ended the call and slipped up the stairs. Gripping the bat in her hands, she paused to listen, searching for the direction of the noise.

It was coming from her room. She scanned the hall, the extra bedroom and bath at the top of the stairs, but they were empty.

Her eyes had adjusted to the dark now, and she peered into her bedroom. The windows were closed, the bed made, nothing amiss. No signs of an intruder.

She crept inside, then realized the cry was coming from her closet. She eased opened the door and her heart clenched.

An infant was kicking and screaming from an infant carrier on the floor, a darling little girl wrapped in a pink blanket.

She knelt and scooped up the child to comfort her, her mind racing. What was going on?

There had been blood downstairs…. Someone was hurt.

The baby's mother?

POLICE CHIEF JOHN WISE gripped his cell phone with his fist as his father lapsed into a diatribe about his plans for John's future.

"You know you were meant to do more than work in that hole-in-the-wall town," his father bellowed. "The most serious crime you've solved has been the theft of those stupid Butterbean dolls. And that was just a bunch of kids selling them on eBay."

John silently cursed. "You don't have to remind me." The case had been the talk of the small town. All the parents had been in an uproar, divided on the issue. Some blew it off as boys being boys while others wanted the kids punished for tainting the town's biggest tourist draw.

CNN had picked up the story, plastered photos of Butterville Babyland Hospital on the news, panning the rooms where the Butterbean babies were birthed from their butterbean shells along with a picture of him in uniform as if he were guarding the dolls. Miss Mazie, the doll's originator, had her five minutes of fame.

And he'd looked like a country bumpkin fool.

"You need to move on," his father continued. "We want the political supporters to take you seriously when your name comes up for office."

Sweat dribbled down his jaw. "I know, Dad. But the town needs me now. Leonard Cultrain has been released from prison and poses a threat." Especially to the women.

His phone beeped that he had another call, and he jumped on it. "A 9-1-1 is coming in. I've got to go."

"What this time? Someone's cat up a tree?" his father said in disgust.

His father was probably right. But he'd heard enough for tonight. "Later." He disconnected the call and clicked to dispatch. "Chief Wise here."

"We just got a call from Samantha Corley's house. An intruder."

He scrubbed a hand over his face, scraping beard stubble. "Did you remind her not to go inside?"

"I told her to stay on the line but then the line went dead."

John swore, then hit the siren, wheeled around and raced toward Samantha's cabin. The damn woman was a magnet for trouble. That job of hers was going to get her killed one day.

Not that he didn't admire her dedication to her calling—and her killer legs—but he wished she'd choose another line of work. Let someone else deal with the parent abusers and troubled families in the county.

But she'd grown up in a foster home, so he guessed it was her nature. Still, sometimes he worried about the blasted woman.

Why, he didn't know. He'd known her since high school, but she'd never given him the time of day. Except for that friend of hers, Honey Dawson, who'd left town months and months ago, Sam hadn't made many friends. And as far as he knew, she'd never had a boyfriend.

He guessed the morons in town couldn't see past that quiet, independent demeanor of hers. That and the gossip about her father being a bad cop, killed because of it.

Coupled with the fact that she was a tough girl from a foster home and that she could outshoot most men in town, she intimidated the hell out of them, too.

But he actually admired her guts and her skill.

His mind ticked over the possibilities of who might want to harm her. Leonard had just been released today and now Sam was in trouble—could the two be connected?

Adrenaline shot through him, and he pressed the gas and sped up. If the son of a bitch had hurt her, he'd be back in the pen tonight. And this time no technicality would get him off.

His heart rate kicked up as he rounded the curve and turned onto Pine Bluff, then raced around the winding road, fighting the curves at breakneck speed. He swung onto the gravel drive leading up the ridge to her cabin on two wheels, bracing himself mentally and physically for what he might find.

He approached the cabin and screeched to a stop, then he grabbed his gun and jumped from the vehicle, scanning the periphery for an intruder, and for Sam. If the fool woman had any sense, she'd have waited outside. But he didn't see an intruder or Sam anywhere.

It figured she'd try to handle things on her own.

He saw a dark green sedan with a dent in the front fender, then noticed the plates were Fulton County and frowned. Why would an intruder have parked in front of the house?

A coyote's wail rent the night, trees rustled in the wind, and an owl hooted. The chill of the night engulfed him, warning him trouble was at hand. Too close by to ignore.

He inched forward, searching the porch, the windows, the doorways for signs of movement, and sounds of an intruder.

When he pushed the front door open, he saw the blood splattered on the kitchen floor, and his chest clenched.

He hoped to hell that wasn't Sam's blood.

Gun at the ready, he crept toward the kitchen but it appeared empty, although the blood trail led out the back door. It looked as if the intruder might have gone into the woods. God, he might have Sam with him.

Then a sound disturbed the quiet. He hesitated, tensed, listening.

A crying baby? He hadn't seen Sam around much; surely she hadn't had a baby without his knowing.

He pivoted to search for the child and realized the cry had come from upstairs. He slowly moved toward the staircase, but glanced in the dining room first just to make sure it was empty. Satisfied the downstairs was clear, he tiptoed up the steps, pausing to listen. If the intruder had Sam up there, he wanted to catch him off guard.

But just as he turned the corner of the staircase, a

shadow moved in front of him. He reacted instantly and raised the gun. "Police, freeze."

A strangled yelp made him pause, then an object swung down. He jumped back to dodge the blow, and the object connected with the floor.

What the hell?

He flipped on the light aiming his gun at the source, then Sam screamed.

His heart hammered. "Sam! For God's sake, I could have shot you."

She pulled back, her eyes huge in her pale face. "John?"

He heaved a breath, trying to control his raging temper. She could have killed him with that damn bat.

"Did you see anyone?" she whispered shakily.

Feeling like a heel for yelling at her, he reached out and stroked her arms. Her dark curly hair was tousled, her cheeks flushed, and fear glimmered in her vibrant brown eyes. "No. It looks like the intruder went out the back door."

"There was blood," she whispered. "Someone's blood...."

He pulled her up against him, surprised at how soft she felt when she was such an athlete, was so well-toned. "I know, but it's all right," he murmured. "I'm here now."

She allowed him to soothe her for a brief second, then Sam suddenly pulled away as if she realized she'd let down her guard and shown a weakness by letting him touch her.

He stiffened. What was wrong with him? He had a job to do, and this was Samantha Corley, Miss Cool and Independent.

Although he had to admit that he'd liked the way she felt up against him.

"I'M SORRY, I WAS JUST SHAKEN for a moment." Sam blushed and squared her shoulders, chastising herself for acting so wimpy. But the thought that the little baby might have been in danger frightened her.

"Don't sweat it," he said. "Let's go sit down and you can tell me what happened."

She nodded, but the little girl whimpered from the bedroom again, and she whirled around. "Let me get the baby."

"Baby?" his gruff voice echoed behind her as he followed her into her bedroom.

He paused at the doorway as if uncomfortable entering her private room, then cleared his throat and walked on in, following her to the closet.

She opened the door, then knelt and scooped up the whimpering child in her arms. "Shh, sweetheart, it's all right. I'll take care of you."

"Good grief, Sam, what's going on? You have a baby in the closet?"

She wrapped the blanket snugly around the child and patted her back as she turned to him. "Whoever was here, the mother maybe, left her in my room."

Shock strained his features for a brief second, then she saw the wheels turning in his mind. "I see."

She swallowed, cradling the infant to her chest, then gestured toward the diaper bag as the little girl began to fuss. "Can you grab that and bring it downstairs? She might be hungry. I'll give her a bottle."

He gave a clipped nod, then yanked the frilly pink bag up with one hand as if it were a snake, and she almost laughed.

She started toward the stairs, but John reached out a

hand to stop her. "Let me go first just in case the intruder decided to return."

Her chest tightened, but she nodded. He braced his gun again as they descended the steps, his gaze scanning the foyer and rooms, but the house appeared to be empty.

She headed to the kitchen, but again he stopped her. "That room is a crime scene now, Sam. You can't go inside."

She bit her lip and jiggled the baby up and down. "But the baby needs to be fed."

He shifted, looking uncomfortable, then glanced into the kitchen, which adjoined the den. "All right. Sit down in the den and tell me what to do. We can't touch the blood or door. I want a crime unit to process the kitchen for forensics."

She nodded, took two steps and settled in the rocking chair, cradling the baby to her and rocking her.

"Let me call for backup first." He phoned the station. "I need a crime scene unit out at Samantha Corley's house along with officers to search the woods." He hesitated and glanced at Sam. "And bring the bloodhounds. We might be looking for a body."

A shudder coursed through her as he disconnected the call. Then he turned to her with a helpless expression as he searched the diaper bag and pulled out a plastic bottle. "No ID or wallet inside. What do I do with the bottle?"

She bit back a laugh. "See if there's formula in the bag."

He dug inside the bag and removed a can, then frowned.

"It's simple, John," Sam said. "Just open the can, fill

the bottle, then heat a pan of water and sit the bottle in it to warm."

John frowned. "Why don't you just use the microwave?"

She looked at him as if he was an idiot. "Because it might get too hot and the formula would burn the baby's throat."

"Oh."

How would he know? With a grim expression, he reached inside the cabinet, removed a saucepan, filled it and turned on the burner. "How long does it heat?"

"A minute or two. You can test it on your arm."

Again, he frowned, then filled the bottle and set it inside the pan. While it heated, he went to his squad car and returned a moment later with a camera and crime kit.

The water had started to boil, so he removed the bottle and brought it over to her. "You check it. I don't know what it's supposed to be like."

She smiled, took the bottle, then shook out a drop of milk on her arm. "Perfect."

The baby began to fuss and latched on to the bottle, and she watched as John photographed the kitchen, the overturned chair, the broken glass on the floor, the blood.

Odd that he seemed far more comfortable working a crime scene than he did with a baby.

He gestured toward the door. "That looks like a woman's earring."

Sam narrowed her eyes and saw the moon-shaped silver earring, and emotions welled in her throat. "Yes, it does. She must have lost it in the struggle."

The baby curled her fingers on the edge of the bottle and Sam stroked her soft, fine blond hair. "The mother must have come to me with the baby because she needed help."

"And whoever was after her followed her," he said in a gruff tone.

Sam glanced at the stream of dark red blood, her insides churning. Had the intruder killed the little girl's mother? Or could she still be alive?

Chapter Two

A half hour later, sirens screeched up the mountainside, vehicles careening to a stop outside Sam's house. John met them, then gestured to the patrol officers, Wilkins and Fritz, who climbed out with the bloodhounds.

"There's evidence of a struggle in the kitchen. Blood," he said specifically. "It appears that the intruder dragged a woman's body into the woods." He paused. "Be careful. This guy might be armed."

Both men nodded, then headed around back and set off into the dense, dark woods with flashlights, the bloodhounds immediately picking up the scent.

"CSI Turner and Akers," a heavyset young guy said, flashing his ID. "Where do you want us?"

"The front door was jimmied, so check for prints there. The kitchen appears to be the main crime scene so process it thoroughly." He flicked a thumb toward Akers. "Follow me around back." Turner began with the front door, while Akers walked behind him. They studied the back porch, then the grass beneath the steps.

John knelt down, brushing dry crushed leaves aside. "Look, there are boot prints. They're big, most likely a male's, and might belong to our perp."

"I'll do a plaster cast of a print," Akers said. "And search for forensics out here."

"Thanks. I'll check the car and run the plates, then it needs to be processed, as well." John glanced at the woods one more time, hoping his guys found something. Preferably the woman alive.

The perp couldn't have gotten too far, not on foot. Unless he had a car hidden down the road. Of course, once he reached the creek, they might lose his trail.

John strode back to the driveway, then called in the license. Five minutes later, he learned the car was registered to a man named Harry Finch from Atlanta.

Hmm, then who was the woman driving the car? His wife?

He pulled on gloves and shined his flashlight inside the sedan. A fast-food wrapper lay on the floor, a soda can in the cup holder, chewing gum wrappers in the ashtray. He snapped a photo of them, then opened the car door and examined the seats and floor. Pollen dotted the windshield, a long blond stray hair was on the dash, a fiber of some kind had caught in the console, and a baby sock the little girl must have kicked off lay on the seat.

He searched the interior but didn't find a purse or wallet. Slipping around to the passenger side, he opened the glove compartment and searched the contents. No wallet or ID, but he found the registration, verifying the car belonged to Finch.

At least that was something to go on.

He bagged the soda can and wrapper, used tweezers to pick up the hair and fiber and bagged them as well as the infant's sock.

Surely the woman had a suitcase of some kind. He popped the trunk and found a small overnight bag stowed inside, so he pulled it out and rummaged through it. A pair of jeans, a lime-green T-shirt, underwear—very frilly underwear—a pair of lime-green flip-flops, toiletries, a pair of boxers and tank shirt for sleeping with the words Hot Stuff on the seat of the boxers.

Not much in the way of clothes—maybe she hadn't planned on staying long.

Or she'd left wherever she was so quickly that she hadn't had time to pack. In fact, the pj's, T-shirt, jeans all looked new and cheap as if she'd just picked them up at a discount store.

Still, he found no ID inside. What in the hell had she done with it?

Ditched it so she couldn't be traced?

Of course. She knew someone was after her, so she'd gotten rid of her ID, used cash. And run here to Sam.

He cursed, his throat working to swallow. And now that the damn perp knew where Sam was, she might be in danger, as well.

He carried the evidence he'd collected to Turner, who was finishing up with the front door. "Take this and process it, and one of you go over the car once you finish with the kitchen. I want the car impounded, as well."

Turner nodded. "I was heading inside now."

"Follow me." John led the way, and Turner went into the kitchen to process it. Sam was still sitting in the rocking chair. The sight of her cuddling the child, looking so protective and loving and—feminine— stirred something deep inside him, and reminded him of a time when he'd thought his girlfriend was pregnant. When he'd been foolish enough to think a woman mattered more than his career.

Never again.

"Shh, sweetie," Sam whispered. "I know you want your mama, but it's going to be all right."

John's chest tightened. He hoped to hell she was right.

But judging from the sight of all that blood, the baby's mother might not be coming back at all.

SAM GLANCED AT JOHN, and her shoulders bunched with nerves. He looked grim and angry, more brooding than she'd ever seen. "Did you find anything?"

John shrugged. "CSI is looking. But there was no ID or purse in the car."

She frowned, but then smiled down at the baby as she sucked greedily on the bottle. "Her name is Emmie," she said softly.

"How do you know?" John asked.

She folded the edge of the pink blanket back, and he read the embroidered lettering. *Peek-a-boo, Emmie.*

At least we know her first name," he said. "Maybe I missed something in the diaper bag."

Emmie drained the bottle, and Sam lifted her to her shoulder, then patted her back. John retrieved the diaper bag, and she watched as he unloaded the contents—diapers, two fuzzy pink sleepers, a plastic duck, rattle, set of plastic keys, three cans of formula, baby wipes, shampoo, lotion and baby socks.

Just enough things to last a night or two, until Sam could get to the store.

"No, nothing," he said. "Not even a credit card or checkbook." With his gloved hand, he removed a small wad of cash that was tucked inside the diaper bag lining.

"She was on the run," Sam said quietly, her heart

aching for the baby girl. "Probably from the baby's father or an abusive man."

John frowned. "We don't know that yet. Hell, she might have kidnapped the kid and was running from the law."

"I haven't heard any Amber Alerts recently, have you?" Sam asked.

"No, but we don't know how long she's been traveling. I'll check the databases and see if a baby girl has been reported missing lately. How old do you think she is?"

The baby burped, and Sam smiled. "About two or three months. She's just starting to hold her head up."

"I'll take your word on it," he said. "I found registration on the car. It belonged to a man named Harry Finch from Atlanta. Do you recognize the name?"

Sam shook her head. "No."

"You want to tell me what happened before I arrived."

Her stomach knotted as the past few hours flashed back. Her expression must have revealed her anxiety, because he stepped closer and pressed a hand to her arm. "Sam, are you all right?"

She exhaled and gathered her courage. "Yes. I was just thinking about earlier. Before I got home…"

"What happened?"

"I saw Leonard Cultrain today," she admitted. "He's trying to get visitation rights to see his son, and the boy's grandparents, his wife's folks, are fighting it."

His brown eyes turned darker as he narrowed them. "Let me guess. He threatened you?"

She shrugged. "He said I'd be sorry I messed with him."

"Dammit, Sam, you can't go antagonizing that man."

"I wasn't," she said, instantly on edge. "But I have a job to do, and that means protecting his son from him.

Little Joey knows Leonard strangled his mother, and is terrified of his father, and so are the grandparents. Joey saw his dad beat his mother more times than I can count."

John hissed. "I know. I took the calls myself." But the patrol officer who'd found Cultrain drunk in his truck the night of the murder had neglected to read the man his rights before arresting him.

Sam gulped back her fear. "Do you think Leonard came here looking for me? That he might have been hiding out and when this woman came in, he mistook her for me?"

John studied her for a long moment, his expression guarded. "I don't know. Judging from the fact that there's no ID in the car, it's more likely that the woman was in trouble. But you can damn well count on the fact that I'm going to pay Cultrain a visit."

"Shh," she said. "There are delicate ears around."

He arched a brow and leaned over her, a teasing glint in his eyes. "Since when did you develop delicate ears, Sam?"

She tensed at how close he was. She could see his beard stubble, smell his masculine scent, feel his breath on her cheek. Of course, he wouldn't think she was delicate.

Or pretty, either.

She gestured toward the baby. "I was talking about Emmie."

His eyes twinkled, then he pulled back and his frown returned. "Oh."

"Thank you, John," Sam said, banishing any fantasies she might harbor about John Wise, and shifting the baby to look into her big eyes. "I can't stand to think that this woman might have been hurt because of me."

"I'll get to the bottom of it," John said. "Meanwhile, what are you going to do with the baby? Put her in foster care?"

The little girl closed her fingers around Sam's, and her heart twisted. "I don't know. I'll keep her tonight, and then decide. Maybe we'll find her mother and I won't have to place her in the system. At least, not yet."

He averted his gaze as if he didn't think she should count on that.

But Sam had to remain optimistic. This precious baby's mother had not abandoned her, at least not willingly. And she didn't want Emmie to end up without a mother as she had.

Or in the system where Sam knew firsthand that anything could happen to her....

THE NEXT TWO HOURS dragged by while forensics finished processing the scene.

"We'll take the blood and prints to the lab," John said. "Maybe they'll help us ID the woman." He glanced at Turner. "Let's take a DNA sample from the baby, too. We might need it to identify the child."

Turner nodded. "I'll take palm and foot prints, too. That might help with identification."

"Good idea." John gestured toward Sam, who was still holding the baby, guarding her like a mother lion would her cub.

Sam's look turned wary. "When you find the mother, she can identify the baby."

"Sam, we don't know for certain that this woman was the baby's mother," John said firmly. "And you know as well as I do that it may take days or even weeks to find this woman. Besides," he continued, "if the mother is dead, we'll need to look for other family members who can take in the child."

A pained look crossed Sam's face, but she complied. The baby fussed as Turner took a DNA swab from the inside of her mouth and took her palm and foot prints.

"Come on, sweetie," Sam said, standing. "We'll go wash off that nasty ink."

She hurried up the steps, then returned a few minutes later with the baby wrapped snugly in the blanket. She'd also tucked one of those silly Butterbean dolls beside her.

"I didn't figure you for a doll kind of girl," John said with a grimace.

Anger glittered in her eyes as if he'd insulted her. "I'm not, but Bitsy doll is special."

God, she'd even named the damn thing. "Bitsy?"

She jutted her chin up defiantly. "Honey gave me her doll the first night I went to live with Miss Mazie, but Miss Mazie stayed up half the night making me one of my own. This is her, Bitsy."

His gut pinched at the slight warble to her voice. Of course, Miss Mazie had given her the doll; it was her trademark. The older woman had started making the handmade cloth dolls—with their faces in the shape of a butterbean—to give to her foster kids. He'd heard the story. The kids were scared, lonely, some traumatized, and she wanted them to have something special to comfort them at night. She'd fabricated a story about how the babies came from butterbeans that she picked especially off the vines, just the way she picked them to come and live with her and be her children.

Sam had only been seven years old when her parents were murdered. Just a child.

A disturbing image of a tiny, vulnerable Sam flashed

in his head. Had Sam been afraid that night? Had she suffered nightmares of her parents' murder?

Outside the wind shook a tree limb against the windowpane, and he saw the beam from a flashlight weaving back toward the house. His men were returning.

Sam noticed them at the same time, and fear clouded her eyes. They stepped out onto the back and met the two officers who'd been combing the woods, the bloodhounds leading the way into the backyard.

"Did you find anything?" John asked.

Officer Wilkins shook his head. "The trail went cold at the creek. The perp probably waded through the water to the road on the east side by River Ridge where he had a car waiting."

Their boots were wet, so they'd obviously followed the trail until it ended. "You saw tire tracks on the road?"

"There were marks on the shoulder in the dirt," Fritz said. "Course they could have been from someone else. You know that's a popular make-out spot for the teens."

John nodded. Still, he'd have the CSI take tire tracks just to be sure they covered all their bases. "You didn't find anything in the woods? A purse or wallet maybe?"

"Not a thing, Chief," Wilkins said, sounding frustrated. "But it's dark as hell out there."

"I know." John gestured toward the panting dogs. "Come back in the morning when it's light and look again. Maybe we'll find something then."

They agreed and went to their patrol car. Larry, the owner of the local tow truck service, arrived and hooked up the car to haul to the impound lot. The CSI team packed up to leave.

He walked Sam back inside, but the stark sight of the

blood made him pause. There was nothing else he could do tonight, not until he heard from forensics.

"Put the baby to bed and I'll clean up here," he said.

"I can clean up," Sam said, that hard look back in her eyes.

"Don't argue," he snapped, irritated that she was so stubborn. "You look exhausted."

"I'm not sure I'll sleep tonight," she admitted.

He wanted to tell her he'd stay and protect her. But getting involved with Samantha Corley was the last thing he needed to do. Just the way she held that baby made him see her in a different light. Sam wanted a family, that was obvious. That was the reason she took care of everyone else.

And he had his own agenda—a career he wanted to build. A family wouldn't be part of it. At least not with a woman whose father was rumored to be a dirty cop. That wouldn't look good for him.

Still, she looked exhausted and had been through hell. "I can stay," he said matter-of-factly.

Her gaze met his, something intense and hot passing between them. Anger?

Attraction?

"Thanks, John," she said, "but I'll be fine. As you pointed out, I'm not exactly delicate. I can take care of myself."

Regret hit him. Had he hurt her by those words? He hadn't meant them as an insult.

"But I will take you up on the offer to clean up the blood," she said. "While you do that, I'll put Emmie down. Then I'll make sure my shotgun is loaded and by my bed."

Leaving off on that note, she turned and strode up the steps, jiggling the baby in her arms. He stood for a second watching her, admiring her. Wishing he didn't find her mixture of tenderness with the baby and her tomboy toughness and tenacity so damn sexy. Wishing he didn't find the sway of those hips so seductive.

He'd clean up the blood and get on his way.

He had a case to solve. And the first stop he was going to make when he left was Leonard Cultrain's house. He'd find out if the bastard had been here tonight.

And if he had, the man would be sorry he'd ever set foot on Sam's land.

Chapter Three

Sam bolted the doors, rocking Emmie back and forth in her arms as John's car disappeared down the driveway. Darkness bathed the exterior of the house and property, the events of the night leaving her shaken and exhausted.

She'd never imagined how violated having an intruder in her home would make her feel, or how instantly she could grow attached to a little baby. But the child snuggled up to her, and her heart melted and warmth spread through her.

"Let's put you to bed," she whispered. "And tomorrow, we'll go into town and buy you a portable crib and more diapers and…"

What was she thinking? She had to file a report, find a temporary foster home for the little girl.

Emmie snuggled deeper against her chest though, and her heart fluttered. Then again, maybe she could just keep the baby until they found her parents or another family member.

She carried Emmie to the guest room across from hers and settled her on the bed, then placed pillows around the edge for safety. Emmie wasn't old enough to crawl, but sometimes babies scooted in their sleep. Then she covered her with the blanket, leaned over and pressed a kiss to the child's forehead.

"Sleep tight, princess. I'll be right across the hall from you." Emmie twisted slightly, her fingers closing around the blanket edge, then slid her thumb in her mouth and began to gently suck it.

Sam smiled, then undressed and pulled on a nightshirt. But the haunting reminder of the violence downstairs sent her to get her shotgun.

She brought it upstairs, then paused to look at the baby from the doorway. The sight of the little girl stirred a longing for a family. For a man to love her and a child to call her own.

A dream she might never have.

She groaned, went to her room, put the gun beside the bed and crawled beneath the covers. But John's offer to stay echoed in her head.

He'd only been doing his job.

John Wise certainly didn't see her as a love interest. The man was a cop through and through. Besides, she'd heard talk that he might leave town to pursue loftier goals.

And Butterville was her home, the only place she'd ever felt safe.

The wind whipped the tree branches against the windowpane, and she tensed.

Except tonight, she didn't feel safe at all.

JOHN ROLLED HIS SHOULDERS to relieve the tension knotting his neck as he drove down the mountain and pulled into Leonard Cultrain's drive. The man had moved back in with his mother in a weathered, clapboard house that had been built at least fifty years ago.

The white paint was chipped, the porch sagging, the screens torn.

Brittle fall leaves crunched beneath his feet as he climbed out, walked up to the front door and knocked. He glanced at the window while he waited, saw a light flicker on in the back room, then heard shuffling. A moment later, Leonard's mother shouted, "Who's there?"

"It's Chief Wise, Miss Cultrain, please open up."

He heard her unlocking the door, then it screeched open and she peered outside through the crack. Her gray bun was falling out of the hairpins, and she clutched an old chenille robe to her neck. "What you want?"

"I need to speak to your son Leonard."

She glared at him, clacking her teeth as her mouth worked side to side. "Do you know what time it is?"

"Yes, ma'am," John said. "But it's important. Is he here?"

She jerked her head sideways. "He's in bed where I was before you pounded on the door."

"Please go get him," John said, struggling for patience, "or I'll come in and do it myself."

She muttered a curse, then slammed the door in his face, and he heard her shuffling to the back calling Leonard's name. "That danged chief of police is here to harass you, Lennie. You tell him we'll sue his ass if he bothers us again."

"Son of a bitch," Leonard snarled so loudly that John braced himself for a confrontation. The burly, tattooed man swung the door open wearing jeans and no shirt, his belly hanging over the waistband of his pants. "I just got home, Chief," he barked. "You the welcome wagon?"

"Where were you tonight?" John asked without preamble.

Leonard's eyes narrowed to slits. "Here having dinner with my mama." He rubbed his belly. "She cooked me fried chicken and biscuits and gravy." He threw a look over his shoulder to where his mother stood like a hawk. "Ain't that right?"

"Sure is. Then we watched the game shows all night."

"Why you asking?" Leonard said.

"Because there was an incident at Samantha Corley's house tonight. I thought you might have been involved."

A leer slid onto Leonard's face. "You did, did you? What kind of incident? Someone hurt the bitch?"

John gritted his teeth. "Actually I believe another woman was attacked in Samantha's house. Heard you had issues with her today."

Anger flashed in Leonard's eyes. "Damn right. That nosy busybody's trying to keep me from my kid, and that ain't right."

As if a murderer deserved to be with his son. "So you went to her house to teach her a lesson?"

A dark laugh boomed from Leonard's chest. "If I had, she'd know it. I wouldn't have settled for someone else."

"He answered your questions," Miss Lou Lou snapped. "Now get out. I need my beauty sleep."

John caught the door before Leonard could slam it in his face. "Stay away from her, Cultrain, or you'll be sorry."

A nasty chuckle rumbled from the bastard. "You tried locking me up and that didn't work."

John shot him an equally evil grin. "Who said anything about jail?"

SAM SPENT THE NEXT MORNING clearing her calendar and arranging for someone to take over her caseload for a few days. She filed a report with social services regarding Emmie, but every time she considered placing the baby in a foster home, memories of her own traumatic experiences flooded her.

She couldn't leave the little girl.

She fed Emmie, bathed her and changed her into the extra sleeper, then made a list of items she needed to pick up in town. But first, she'd stop by and see John.

Chief Wise, not John. Remember, he's a cop.

She settled the baby into the infant carrier, and fit it into the car seat base, smiling as the little girl clutched the Butterbean doll in her hand. "I know Bitsy is soft. She's your new best friend, isn't she, sweetie?"

Emmie cooed and batted her little fist at Sam, and Sam's heart melted again.

Ten minutes later, she parked at the police station, took Emmie from the car and wrapped the blanket around her to ward off the fall chill as she hurried inside. One of the deputies, Deputy Floyd, a blond guy in his early twenties, smiled at her from his desk. She'd met him before on another case.

"Hello, Sam."

"Hi, Phil. Is John…I mean Chief Wise here?"

He nodded. "In his office. You can go on back."

"Thanks."

"Hey, I heard about the trouble last night. Are you all right?"

"Yes, thanks." She cradled the baby to her and went to John's office, pausing to drink in his features through the glass partition separating the space. He was at least six foot three, his body muscular, his shoulders broad, his hands big. His hair was dark and thick, his eyes an amber-brown like scotch.

But his expression was somber as he talked into the phone.

He glanced up and spotted her, his eyes narrowing slightly, then he waved her in.

"Thanks. Let me know if you find anything in those woods." He hung up, then scrubbed a hand over his chin. "I just sent two officers out to search the forest behind your house again."

"Any news on the missing woman?"

He shook his head. "Not yet. I just talked to the lab, and they're supposed to fax over anything they find. I asked them to run the prints first. If she's in the system, we might get a hit."

"I hope so." Sam glanced down at Emmie, praying the woman was alive.

John clenched his jaw, tension rippling between them. "I went by Leonard Cultrain's house last night."

Sam's breath caught. "What did he say?"

"He obviously has a grudge against you," he said in a gruff tone. "But, his damn mother gave him an alibi."

"That figures. She's pretty bitter."

He gave a clipped nod. "I don't care. If we find his prints at your house, or if those boot prints are his size, I'll bring him in." He closed the distance between them. "I warned him to stay away from you, so if he gives you any trouble, call me."

"I will." Emmie began to fuss, and Sam jiggled her up and down, soothing her with soft whispers.

John's gaze darkened. "What did you decide to do about the baby?"

"I rearranged my calendar so I can take off a few days. That way, I can take care of her myself."

John frowned. "Are you sure that's a good idea?"

She stiffened. "You don't think I can take care of a baby?"

He cursed under his breath. "Dammit, Sam, stop being so defensive. I just thought you'd put her in foster care."

Sam bit her lip. If Mazie was still taking in kids, she might. But the other two homes she used were full. And Emmie was so tiny.... "She's been through enough. Hopefully you'll find her parents, and it will only be for a few days."

"I guess you know what you're doing." He shifted, then rapped his knuckles on the desk. "I checked the hospitals and morgue but found nothing. Of course, if the woman is dead, the perp could have dumped her body anywhere in the mountains. She might not be found for days."

A tense silence stretched between them, filled with the things he hadn't said. That with the isolated areas in the mountains, the body might never be found.

His phone rang, and he reached for it. She started toward the door, but he gestured for her to wait. "Chief Wise. Yeah? What did you find?" He paused and scribbled something down on a notepad. "I see. Thanks."

"What?" Sam asked as he disconnected the call.

"That was the Atlanta PD. They traced the owner of the car the woman was driving. Harry Finch was out of town, but flew back into Atlanta yesterday and discovered his car had been stolen."

Sam's throat thickened as a dozen different scenarios raced through her head. "The poor woman. She must have been desperate."

His mouth twisted into a grimace. "Either that or she's a criminal. Maybe she kidnapped the baby, as well."

Sam hugged the baby closer to her chest. She didn't want to think Emmie had been kidnapped, but she had to admit that anything was possible.

She'd protect her until they found out.

As soon as Sam left, John checked national police databases and the National Center for Missing and Exploited Children, searching photos and names for hours. By late afternoon, his search hadn't turned up a lead, and he was getting antsy, so he decided to drive to the newly built lab that serviced the North Georgia area and push them to run the forensics tests.

On the drive, he checked with the officers who'd searched the woods again, but their search had yielded nothing new. A half hour later, he entered the concrete building and walked straight to the lab.

CSI Turner met him. "Chief Wise."

"I need the results of the forensics evidence your team brought in."

"The blood will take time." Turner gestured for him to follow him to the computer. "I was just about to run the prints from the front door. There are three different ones and so smudged, I'm not sure we'll get a match."

"Exclude Samantha Corley's," John said, stating the obvious.

Turner nodded and fed in the other two. "This one is a male's," Turner said. But a half hour later, they hadn't found a match.

"He must not be in the system," John said. Meaning he hadn't been arrested, didn't have a government job, and he hadn't served in the military. Not much to go on, but it might help.

"Check the ones from the car," John said. "I want to know who this woman is."

John claimed the seat beside him and watched Turner feed the prints into the system. Print after print flashed onto the screen, the computer doing its magic, placing them side by side then overlaying them to see if they matched.

"Did you run the baby prints yet?"

"Sorry, we're backed up. But I'll get someone on it ASAP." He made a clicking sound with his teeth. "Did you check Atlanta hospitals?"

"Yeah," John said wearily. "Although we have no idea if that's where the baby was born. For all we know this woman could have crossed a half dozen state lines before she reached Atlanta. The car that she drove to the house was stolen. We could be looking at a mother in trouble, or a kidnapped baby."

Turner jerked his gaze toward him. "You receive any Amber Alerts?"

John shook his head. "No, and you'd think if someone's little girl was taken, they'd have gone to the police."

"Could be a custody issue."

John nodded. Domestic issues turned violent all the time. And this one might have led to a murder.

The computer flashed, and Turner clicked a few keys to highlight the information. "We've got a match."

John's heart hammered in his chest. The print belonged to a woman all right.

A woman he knew.

Honey Dawson.

Holy hell. How was he going to tell Samantha that the missing woman was her best friend?

SAM GATHERED BABY SLEEPERS, outfits, socks, diapers, bottles, formula, wipes, soap and powder, washcloths, a hooded towel and various other items she thought she might need. She also purchased a baby sling and a portable crib, rationalizing that she could always donate it to a charity once she didn't need it anymore.

Or keep it for herself.

Her lungs tightened as she drew in a breath. Not that she had hope of having a baby anytime soon. That would require a man.

At least for her, it would. Other women chose alternative means, but she was old-fashioned. She wanted the whole nine yards. The man, the romance, the proposal first.

The family that she'd once had and lost.

Of course, getting pregnant also required sex, and she was inexperienced in that area and had no prospects in sight.

Unless she decided to adopt....

What if the little girl's mother was dead and she had no family who wanted to take her in?

Stop, Sam. You learned long ago not to get too attached.

The baby cooed, and she patted her back, juggled her purse to retrieve her credit card and paid for her purchases, then hurried to the car. Emmie began to fuss, and Sam sang her a lullaby as she fastened her in the car seat, then tipped the young man who was loading the supplies into the trunk of her SUV.

It was growing dark, storm clouds brewing on the horizon. She needed to get home. She didn't want to be driving with Emmie in the car during one of the notorious thunderstorms famous in the South.

The baby kicked the blanket off her feet, and Sam adjusted it, then climbed in the driver's seat, started the car and wove from the parking lot through town. Fall leaves fluttered from the trees as the gusty wind picked up, and car lights dotted the small town, the tourists already pouring in for the upcoming fall festival and to see the array of colorful leaves.

As she turned onto the narrow winding road leading toward her cabin, car lights blinded her from behind. She tensed, slowing around the curve, but the car sped up, zooming on her tail.

Then suddenly it slammed into her rear. What was happening? Was the car out of control?

He sped up, tires screeching then rammed into her again. Sam gritted her teeth, grasping the steering wheel with a white-knuckled grip. The crazy fool—he was going to get them all killed.

A chill slithered up her spine at the thought, then the truth hit her. What if the driver was the same person who'd been in her house the night before?

Dear God, he knew where she lived. But why come back for her?

Emmie piped up, and she suddenly realized that he knew she had the baby.

He was after Emmie. And he'd kill her to get the child. Would he kill the baby, too?

Chapter Four

Sam silently cursed the man trying to run her off the road, jerked the wheel to the right to avoid careening into the embankment then swung the car onto the graveled drive toward her house.

The baby wailed from the backseat as if she sensed the danger, and Sam sped up, glancing over her shoulder at the lights bearing down on her.

"He's not going to hurt you, little one," she said over her shoulder. "Don't worry. I'll protect you and find your mama."

But the man sped up, too, moving closer on her tail.

She hit the accelerator, shooting forward, and he lost control for a moment and skimmed a tree. The skid gave her just enough time to throw the car into park, grab the baby from the backseat and race inside.

She slammed the door, put the baby carrier on the floor then grabbed her shotgun. Outside, the sound of the car roared nearer, gears and tires grinding, then the engine died and a door slammed.

Emmie wailed louder, kicking her feet and waving her fist, and Sam's temper rose. Why would someone want to hurt this baby?

Sam's hands shook as she moved the curtain aside and glanced out the window. She needed to call 9-1-1, but there wasn't time. The dark sedan was parked off the drive by a thick pocket of trees, and the silhouette of a man slithered through the shadows, creeping toward the side window.

"I'll be right back, sweetie," she said softly. She slowly opened the door, then inched outside onto the porch and around toward the side. The man was crouching low in the bushes, weaving toward the window. The sound of glass shattering sounded over the wind. Panic hit her again.

He was trying to break in.

Her insides knotted. She had to protect the baby. "You're not going to get to Emmie," she muttered as she raised the gun, braced it against her hip and aimed. The bushes rustled, wind whipping through the trees, but she fired at the bushes, gritting her teeth at the kick.

A curse rent the air, the bushes rustled again and she fired a second shot. Another curse echoed through the wind, then the man jumped up and ran toward the woods and his car. She fired again, determined he know she meant business. The shell pinged off the gravel near his feet. He jumped into the car, started the engine, swung the car around and tore down the drive, slinging gravel in his wake.

She was trembling, but waited until he disappeared then ran inside and locked the door. Emmie was crying harder, her cheeks red, her sniffles twisting Sam's heart.

She scooped the precious baby into her arms and began to soothe her. "Shh, sweetheart, it's all right. The bad man is gone now."

But she had a sinking feeling he would be back.

She stroked Emmie's back, swaying her gently in her arms and pacing frantically in front of the window to make sure the man didn't return as she dialed 9-1-1 again.

AT JOHN'S REQUEST, the lab confirmed that the blood on the floor of Sam's house was Honey's. They still had to compare the baby's blood and DNA with Honey's. Meanwhile, John had to tell Samantha Corley what he'd learned, that it was Honey's blood on her floor.

His phone buzzed on his way to her house, and he snapped it open. "Chief Wise."

"Chief, a 9-1-1 call just came in from Samantha Corley's house."

Again? Dammit.

He scrubbed his hand over his face. "What now?"

"She said someone tried to run her off the road and followed her to her house."

He adjusted his holster and weapon, grabbed his jacket and rushed to the door. "I'm on my way."

John flipped on the siren and raced toward Sam's. The wind beat at his car as he swerved around slower traffic, beeped at a truck to move over and let him by, then swung onto the mountain road leading to her place.

Five minutes later, he veered onto her driveway, scanning the woods as he flew up her drive and scanned the perimeter of her property. Dark clouds hung heavy in the night, the threat of bad weather ominous.

He screeched to a stop behind her car, wielded his gun in case the perp was lurking around, then walked toward the porch, his senses alert. Trees rustled, an animal howled and the ping of falling rocks echoed from the neighboring woods.

He climbed the steps, then knocked. "Samantha, it's John."

His pulse raced as he waited, but finally he heard the lock shifting and the door opened with a screech.

The sight of Sam terrified and holding a baby in her arms made his chest clench and pulled at heartstrings he didn't know he had.

Heartstrings he'd only felt one other time—years ago when he thought his high school girlfriend was carrying his baby. He'd been willing to sacrifice his career and dreams to do right by the child, but his father had called him a fool. His father was right. Later he'd learned that the girl had lied to him, that the baby wasn't his.

Since then his trust in women was shot.

He'd vowed to focus on his goals, never to let a woman sidetrack him again.

But Sam, who fought so hard to protect others, especially children, was shaking and terrified. Not for herself, either. That was obvious.

She was frightened for the innocent little girl in her arms.

He couldn't help himself. He stepped inside, shut the door behind him then pulled her up against him. "Are you okay?" he asked gruffly.

She leaned against him, a testament to her emotional state, and sighed against his chest. "Some man tried to run me off the road," she whispered hoarsely. "He followed me home, then tried to break in the window."

Anger surged through him, and he tightened his grip on her, the baby calming as the two of them held her between them.

"It's all right now," he said. "I'll catch this SOB."

She pulled away slightly, composing herself, her eyes tormented. "John, I think he wants the baby."

John's jaw tightened. "What makes you think that? It could have been someone else, some man disgruntled from one of your cases. Don't forget that Leonard Cultrain is out of jail and has a grudge against you."

She frowned. "It wasn't Leonard. Think about it, John. Last night a woman was hurt here in my house. But I didn't see the man and can't identify him, so why come after me?" She turned a panicked look up at him. "He wanted Emmie, John, and he came back to get her. I think he might hurt her, too, just like he did the mother. That's the reason the woman hid the baby in my closet."

His blood ran cold. If this maniac hurt the baby, it would be over John's dead body.

She paced away, rocking the little girl in her arms with such love that again John's chest clenched.

Sam would make a wonderful mother.

He had to tell her the truth about Honey.

But hearing that her best friend might have stolen this child, or if the baby was hers, that they were in danger, wouldn't be easy.

And the worst-case scenario—Honey might be dead.

SAM TOOK A CALMING BREATH, grateful for John's presence. Slowly her adrenaline was waning, and Emmie was starting to whimper again and needed to be fed.

"Let me get her a bottle," she said.

"We need to talk, but go ahead and take care of the baby first," John said. "I'll check the window for prints and forensics, then board it up for the night."

She nodded. "There's some extra plywood and a hammer in the garage."

He nodded, and she hurried into the kitchen with the baby while he went outside. She felt his absence in the room the moment he stepped away from her. When he'd pulled her up against him and cradled her and Emmie, she'd felt protected.

Maybe for the first time in her life.

Which was a fantasy. She couldn't rely on anyone else—she had to stand on her own.

She always had.

Except for Honey—when the doe-like girl had befriended her years ago, Sam had clung to her sweetness. The two of them had bonded over lost families, a lack of love and the toughness they'd been forced to adopt to survive.

Memories of high school flooded her as she heated the bottle, hugged the baby to her and watched her eat, her tiny hand gripping Sam's as if she was afraid she would lose her, too.

"I don't know where your mama is, precious, but I'll take care of you until she comes back."

A pain seized her chest. What if Emmie's mother didn't return? What if she was lost, hurt?

Even dead?

No, she couldn't think like that. The baby's mother was coming back. John would find her and reunite them.

Her pulse spiked. When had she ever trusted, or had faith in, a man?

But she instinctively knew that John was the real deal. He would do what he said. He'd been a hero in the town when they were young, a football star.

And the boy every girl had wanted.

His father had been a politician and had pushed him hard.

And although she'd never admitted it, she'd secretly harbored a crush on the guy herself.

But boys had paid no attention to her. She was awkward and shy, not like Honey who was vivacious and sweet and feminine. Despite her background, Honey turned all the boys' heads and had made varsity cheerleader her freshman year.

Odd though that John was one of the few guys in school who'd never hit on Honey.

Of course, he'd never paid attention to *her*, either. Why should he now?

His family had money and prestige where she was just one of the foster kids everyone pitied. The gossip about her father being a dirty cop, causing his own wife's death, haunted her, as well.

Honey had been the only one who'd understood....

The door squeaked open and she froze, her nerves on alert, but she breathed out in relief when John poked his head in. "It's me, Sam."

She pressed a finger to her lip gesturing for him to be quiet, then eased the baby into her infant seat to sleep. Tonight she'd put together the portable crib so the sweet child would have a bed.

"I took a plaster cast of the footprint near the window," John said. "It looks similar to the one from last night, so you may be right. This may be the same guy who attacked the baby's mother. But there weren't any fingerprints so he must have worn gloves."

"You think he's a professional of some kind?"

John shrugged. "I don't know yet. Anyone who watches crime shows these days knows to wear gloves."

"True." Which made his job harder.

"Did you see what kind of car he was driving?"

She shook her head. "No, it looked like some kind of dark sedan, but he was behind me and his lights were blinding."

"You said he rammed into you intentionally?"

She nodded. "Yes, at least twice. I was afraid we might go over the side of the mountain."

"I'll see if he left paint from his car on yours and take a sample." Her eyes clouded over as if she was reliving the scene, and he rubbed her arms with his big hands. "I'll find him, Sam, I promise," he said. "Just give me time."

She stared into his eyes and the tension seeped from her, yet another kind of tension vibrated between them. She longed to have him hold her again.

Then his gaze turned hooded, his jaw tightened and a wary expression darkened his face. "Sam?"

Alarm rippled through her. "What is it, John? Did you find something?"

He nodded. "Let's sit down."

Her pulse spiked, but she allowed him to lead her to one of the kitchen chairs. He claimed the one opposite her and planted his beefy fists on his knees. "I did get some interesting results from the fingerprints in the car from last night."

She swallowed, nerves tingling as she realized he thought the news would upset her. "Whom do they belong to?"

A muscle ticked in his jaw, then he cleared his throat. "Your friend Honey Dawson."

Sam's breath caught. Honey? Honey had driven the car here?

Pain and panic ripped through her as she remembered the blood on the floor in her kitchen.

Dear Lord…Honey must have been in trouble and she'd come to her for help.

But why hadn't Honey told her she was pregnant? And who would want to hurt Honey?

She jerked her head toward the infant seat. And the baby… The little girl had baby fine, soft blond hair. And those green eyes…

Was Emmie Honey's little girl?

JOHN SAW THE WHEELS TURNING in Samantha's mind and knew she assumed the baby was Honey's. But he was a cop and he had to go on facts.

And the facts were stacking up against Honey.

"Emmie is Honey's," Sam said with newfound awe in her eyes as she stroked the baby's soft curls.

"We can't say that for certain," John said. "Remember, the car was stolen." He paused, knowing Sam wouldn't like his train of thought, but he was a cop and had to look at the facts. "Honey might have stolen the baby, too. Maybe this guy is trying to recover the child for himself or for the parents."

"No. That's crazy. Honey would never kidnap a child." Sam's dark brown eyes flashed with anger, and her shoulders snapped up in a defensive gesture. "This is Honey's little girl. She looks just like her."

"DNA will have to tell us that, Sam," John said. "Until then, we can't make assumptions."

Sam laid a hand on the baby seat as if she expected him to tear the little girl from her. "Honey would never steal a child, John. I know her. And Emmie—I should have known. Honey always talked about naming her kids after Dallas Cowboy players. Emmit was one of the famous running backs during the Dallas Cowboys' glory days."

"Look, Sam, I understand she was your best friend, but it's obvious that Honey was in trouble. She's been gone over a year now. You have no idea what kind of mess she's gotten herself into."

Sam folded her arms. "I know Honey would have to be desperate to steal a car. That she came to me for help and I wasn't here for her."

John silently cursed. "Sam, you can't blame yourself for what happened to Honey."

"What did happen to her? I saw all that blood," Sam said, her tone full of terror. "Do you think that man…that he killed her, John?"

He hesitated, hated to give her hope and then have her disappointed. But he also hated to squash that hope. "I don't know," John said. "But at least we know who we're looking for. I'll file a missing persons report on Honey, and hopefully someone will come forward with information."

She nodded, stroking the baby's cheek with her finger, tears welling in her eyes. "I hope so, John. Honey wouldn't want her little girl to grow up without a mother."

The pain of Sam's past reverberated in her voice, and his heart squeezed. Sam had always seemed so strong, tough, a fighter.

Anger stirred inside his belly. It was just like Honey to create a mess, then expect Sam to clean it up for her. "Honey came here because she knew you'd take care of her, Sam," John said. "Just like you did when you were younger."

Sam's gaze swung to his, emotions brimming in her eyes, but the old fight returned. "We took care of each other, John. When I first went to the orphanage, Honey was the one who befriended me. Without her I would have been totally lost."

He doubted that but he refrained from arguing.

"We'll find her, John. I just know she's alive." She pressed her hand to her chest. "I'd feel it if she was really gone."

He studied her for a long moment, then swallowed. "Okay, we have work to do. How long has it been since you've seen or spoken to Honey?"

Sam twisted the corner of her mouth up in thought. "On the phone? A few months, although she didn't tell me about her pregnancy. I should have called her more often..."

"Stop it," John said. "Honey chose to leave, Sam. We just have to figure out where she was and what happened to make someone want to kill her."

"DID YOU GET THE BABY?"

He paced across the dingy room, sweating. "No, Honey stashed her at some old friend's house and the bitch got away from me."

A litany of curses exploded on the other end of the line. "You have to kill the bitch and get that baby."

"She's got the sheriff on the case now," he stammered. "Some local yokel who must have known Honey and the Corley woman."

"Kill the cop, too, if he gets in the way. I want that brat out of the picture for good along with anyone else who might ask questions."

Chapter Five

"We have to find Honey. Emmie needs her," Sam said. "Where do we start?"

John checked the clock. "It's late, Sam. Why don't you put the baby to bed for the night? I'll make a call to file that missing persons report."

She nodded. "I bought a baby bed today. I need to put it together."

John gave her a wary look. "Tell me where it is and I'll take care of it."

"The baby things are in the car. I haven't had a chance to bring them in." She stood and brushed the palms of her hands on her hips. "I can get them."

"Sam," John said, his patience snapping as his gaze fell to those voluptuous hips. He needed air. Bad. "I said I'd do it."

She lifted her chin, then paused. "All right. Have you eaten?"

He shook his head. They should talk about food because he suddenly felt hungry for something else.

Something he couldn't have.

Like a taste of Samantha Corley's stubborn mouth.

Oblivious to the torture she was putting him through,

she said, "I'll heat some soup for us. After we get Emmie settled, maybe we can come up with a plan."

After *we* get her settled?

He didn't want any part of the settling, didn't want to get close or attached to that baby or her.

She glanced toward the oak desk in the corner. "I'll see if I can dig up the postcards and letters Honey sent me. Maybe something in them will tell us where she's been and lead to the person after her."

"Good idea."

He removed his phone and punched in the number for the station while he headed out to her car. "Deputy Floyd, I want you to file a missing persons report on a woman named Honey Dawson. She lived in town years ago. Her prints were found on Samantha Corley's door."

"I'll get right on it, Chief. Anything else?"

John glanced back at the house. "Yeah. Someone tried to run Samantha off the road tonight. I think whomever it was hurt Honey and wants the baby. I'm going to stay here tonight to make sure the guy doesn't return. Call me if something comes up."

"Will do, boss."

John hung up, then opened the trunk of the SUV and shook his head at the assortment of baby paraphernalia. "Hell, Sam, what'd you do? Buy out the whole damn store?'

He reached for a giant box of diapers with a grimace, then a case of canned formula and carted them inside, dumping them in the foyer. More bags contained everything from baby clothes, wipes and rattles to a plastic bathtub, something called a mobile, a baby swing, a fold-up stroller and then the portable crib.

The scent of homemade soup wafted toward him,

and his stomach growled. But first things first. He had to put that damn baby bed together. He hoped to hell the instructions were written in English.

Sam met him in the foyer and began to sort out the items, carrying the formula to the kitchen while he carted the box with the bed up the steps to her guest room.

Sam whisked in and began to unload the baby clothes while he tore open the box, pulled out the instructions and started to piece together the bed. The sight of Sam placing tiny baby socks and cuddly sleepers in the drawer made his stomach feel funny.

This scene felt way too domestic—and cozy—to suit him. Sam was actually humming. Humming, for God's sake.

He lowered his head, trying to ignore this soft feminine side of her. Sam had always been a tomboy.

Hell, the tigress had shot at her attacker earlier and scared the damn man off.

And right now, she was scaring the hell out of him because he was beginning to actually like being with her.

No, he wouldn't let this get personal. He'd protect her and the child until they found out what happened to Honey and if the baby was actually hers.

Then Sam could do whatever she wanted, and he'd move on with his plans to leave Butterville.

SAM FROWNED AS SHE STOWED the last of the baby clothes in the drawer.

She'd never had any experience with men, and she certainly didn't understand John's behavior. One minute he'd held her and acted protective, and the next he was growling and practically spitting at the baby furniture.

She walked over and squatted down, then picked up one of the legs to the crib. "John, why are you being such a bear? I told you that you don't have to do this. I'm perfectly capable of putting the bed together myself."

He glared up at her. "I told you I'd do it and I will."

"Then why are you so pissed off?"

His jaw tightened. "I'm just not comfortable around babies."

She frowned. "Well, no one is asking you to play father here. I told you I can take care of myself and Emmie."

"That's right, Sam, you always take care of everyone else," he muttered. "No one takes care of you because you won't let them."

His anger didn't make sense. "In the first place, no one has ever taken care of me because no one has ever *wanted* to," she snapped back.

His gaze met hers, and something odd flickered between them, a moment that felt way too sexual. A hungry look flashed in his eyes, a look she'd seen other men use with Honey but not on her.

A second later it vanished, and she was certain she'd imagined it.

"I don't understand you at all, John."

He shook his head irritably. "I'm sorry, Sam. I didn't mean to bark at you. I just don't like this situation."

"Then leave."

He grabbed her hand and yanked her down to stare into his eyes. "I'm not leaving you two alone," he said in a gruff voice. "Not until we find out who's after the baby."

Her heart fluttered with that odd feeling again, and for some insane reason, she leaned forward, an ache stirring inside her. She wanted him to kiss her.

His gaze met hers, then he lifted his hand and slid it to the back of her neck as if to pull her closer, to give her what she wanted.

But a soft cry shattered the silence and Sam jerked away. Emmie needed her.

She couldn't get used to John being around, not when he had another agenda and planned to leave town.

Besides, he'd made it plain and clear that babies wouldn't be part of his future.

And now she'd held Honey's little girl, she knew a baby would be in her future. If not Emmie, then she would have one of her own or adopt a child.

And John would not be in the picture.

JOHN STARED AT THE SLEEPING baby as she snuggled into her new bed, a tight feeling in his chest. Sam covered Emmie with a pink blanket, then tucked that damn Butterbean doll up to her and kissed her gently.

The fool woman was already getting attached to the child.

Something he couldn't allow himself to do. His future didn't include a wife or kids. At least not one in this town.

She took a baby monitor from a box and placed it on the dresser, then motioned to him to follow, and they went back down the stairs. She set the speaker for the baby monitor on the kitchen counter. "This way I can hear her if she wakes up."

He nodded, watching silently as she dipped them bowls of the steaming soup and placed fresh bread on the table. John had never had dinner with Sam and this homey setting was doing odd things to him, making him want things he'd never wanted before.

Like spending a night with Sam.

"It's not fancy," Sam said. "But it's hot."

"It looks great," he said and meant it.

A small smile curled her mouth, the stress lines relaxing, and he realized he'd never really seen her smile. Sam had always been such a serious girl and student, always on the defensive as if she'd had to fight to survive.

She had, he thought with a stab of remorse for what her young life must have been like. Her parents murdered before her eyes. Her father's name tainted by the gossip about him being a dirty cop. Growing up in an orphanage.

And the kids at school...sometimes they could be cruel. Had been cruel to her and Honey. But Sam had survived and now helped others.

"While you were upstairs, I dug up the old post-cards and letters I received from Honey over the past year," she said. "There aren't many, but I thought they might help."

He sat down and dug into the soup. "This is great, Sam."

She shrugged. "I like to cook."

His gaze met hers and he smiled. "I guess you learned how to when you were young, didn't you?"

She shrugged again and tore off a piece of bread. "Miss Mazie had an expression—you play the cards you've been dealt."

"Even if you've been dealt a crappy hand?"

"It's better than giving up and feeling sorry for yourself."

"You're right. You and Honey never did that, did you?"

"There's no point in it." Sadness tinged her eyes.

"Honey acted tough, but she's a kitten beneath. I always thought she jumped from one guy to the other because she desperately wanted love."

And Sam avoided relationships because she was afraid of getting close to anyone? Of losing them?

He couldn't go there; it was too personal.

Sam picked up one of the postcards from the stack on the table and examined it. "When Honey left here, she had such big dreams. She wanted to be a Dallas Cowboy cheerleader." She sipped her iced tea. "She would have been fantastic, too."

"What happened?"

"I don't know. In her letters she talked about traveling and the men she met."

She paused, as if realizing she was painting her friend in a negative light.

"What if Honey did escape last night?" John asked. "Is there anyone here in town other than you who she would call or go to for help?"

Sam tapped the postcard against the table. "Maybe Dwayne Hicks. He always had the hots for Honey."

John nodded, faintly remembering the two of them dating. "Didn't Dwayne leave town with Honey?"

"Yes," Sam said. "But he came back a couple of months later."

John chewed his bread. "Tomorrow I'll have a talk with Dwayne and see if he's heard from Honey. Maybe he knows what's going on with her."

Sam leaned her head on her hand. "I don't know if they kept in touch, but it's worth a try."

"He couldn't be the baby's father, could he?" John asked.

Sam shook her head. "No, the timing is off. He came

back here months before she would have been pregnant with Emmie."

"We need to find out who the baby's father is," John said. "He might be the one who followed Honey here and tried to kill her."

SAM PUT HER SPOON DOWN, unable to eat any more. Honey had to be alive. She wouldn't, *couldn't* believe that she was gone.

John scowled. "But that's only one scenario, Sam. For all we know, Honey got involved with a bunch of thugs or another lover she left behind was pissed and wanted to hurt her. Or maybe she owed someone money."

"Honey wasn't bad," Sam said, her claws coming out. "She just wanted affection."

John narrowed his eyes and Sam tensed. He had no idea what life had been like for her and Honey.

"I'm not going to argue with you over Honey's virtues," John said. "So stop being defensive, Sam. I'm just trying to find her, and to do that I have to consider every possibility."

Sam sighed and gave him an apologetic look. "I'm sorry. Not knowing where she is, if she's all right, it's just so…hard, John."

John leaned over and placed his hand over hers. His warmth immediately seeped through her, making her feel tingly inside. And safe again.

"Just trust me and let me find the truth."

His gruff tone soothed her nerves. She'd never been close to a man before, but she did trust him. "All right. I'll look through the postcards and letters after I clean the dishes and see if there's someone she met who might know something."

"Good idea," John said. "I'll call the local hotels and inns and see if there are any strangers in town. And tomorrow I'll have my men search any abandoned cabins or houses around the area."

Sam clenched his hand. "These hills have so many hiding holes."

"I know, but it's a start. I promise, Sam, we'll do everything we can to find Honey."

Sam nodded. She wouldn't allow herself to think that Honey was dead.

But Honey was likely injured, had lost blood, and she might be lying in a ditch somewhere or in the woods, bleeding and cold and in serious condition.

She prayed they found her alive so they could bring her safely home to her baby daughter.

Chapter Six

John phoned the station headquarters to alert them that he wanted a team ready for the morning to search the foothills of the mountains. Sam retreated upstairs carrying the postcards Honey had sent her.

Worry assaulted him. He hoped Sam was right. That Honey wasn't a baby snatcher or a criminal. That she'd stolen that car in desperation to escape a man from hurting her child as Sam suggested, not because she was on some wild attempt to get attention and escape a kidnapping charge.

Another possibility—she'd wanted to keep the child from her own father, not because he posed a danger to her or the little girl, but because she wanted to hurt him or was ready to throw him away as she had the other men in her life....

The clock struck midnight, and he couldn't do any more tonight, so he stretched out on Sam's sofa and tried to sleep. But upstairs he heard Sam moving around and the shower kicked on.

He cursed and closed his eyes, trying to banish the images bombarding him. Images of Sam undressing, her bare breasts perky and high, her hips flaring enticingly, her soft skin glistening beneath the spray of the warm water.

Dammit. He pressed his hand over his forehead, trying to gain control. He couldn't believe he was fantasizing about Samantha Corley's sexy body. Not tough, tenacious, tigress Sam.

Not soft, sultry, caring, warm, wonderful Sam.

He rolled over and punched the pillow in disgust. This case was getting to him.

All the more reason he had to solve it quickly and get the hell out of Butterville before he completely lost his sanity and fell for the blasted woman.

No, that would never happen. He wouldn't allow any woman to destroy his future or keep him in this town.

SAM SHOWERED AND PULLED ON a warm flannel gown, then gathered Honey's correspondence and sorted them by chronological order from when she'd received them so she could follow Honey's journey across the States.

Too wired to sleep, she was unnerved by the thought of John being downstairs in her house. She had to distract herself so she wouldn't give in to temptation and go back downstairs to be near him.

You are pathetic, Sam. He's not interested in you personally.

She skimmed the first card, one Honey had sent from Memphis where she and Dwayne had taken a side trip.

Hi, Sam,

Dwayne and I visited Graceland today. It was so awesome. I saw Elvis's house and his costumes, and then we went line dancing! Wish you were here!

From there, Honey had gone to Montgomery, Alabama.

Sam, We ran out of money here, so decided to stay a while. I got a waitressing job at a place called Billy Bob's Barbeque. It's a dive, but there's a hot guy who works there. Dwayne wants us to come back to Butterville. But I'm on my way to Dallas just as soon as I save up some money, with him or without him.

You and I should have taken a road trip long ago. It's amazing!

A few weeks later, Honey had sent a card from Shreveport, Louisiana.

Hi, Sam! Well, I left Montgomery and Randy, the hot guy I'd met at Billy Bob's, and I stopped in Shreveport. I'm going to visit New Orleans before I go on to Dallas. I can't believe there's a big old world out here and we haven't seen any of it!

Sam flipped to the next one.

Hi, Sam. You won't believe it but I'm in Dallas, and I went to watch the cheerleaders today! My God, it was so wonderful. I'm signing up for tryouts and pray I make it.

I also have other news. I met this sexy guy, and I'm in love! Yes, me, Honey Dawson, I'm actually in love. I think he's the one, Sam. I really do.

Maybe you'll get to see me on TV with the cheerleaders one day and in a wedding gown!

Sam sighed and pinched the bridge of her nose. "Oh, Honey," Sam whispered. "What went wrong? You sounded so excited, like you were on top of the world."

But shortly after that the postcards had stopped coming.

Exhaustion and the tension of the day were wearing on her. She placed the postcards on her nightstand and turned out the light. Emmie would probably wake early, and she needed to get some sleep.

Her muscles felt sore from where the car had rammed into her and jerked her around. She closed her eyes, trying to banish the memory.

But downstairs, she heard John's footfalls as he walked around. He'd promised to protect her and Emmie and find out what happened to Honey.

And she trusted and believed him.

But he wasn't convinced that the baby was Honey's child.

Sam knew Emmie belonged to Honey though; she felt it in her bones when she held the baby.

She rolled sideways and closed her eyes, but she couldn't fall asleep for wondering where Honey was, if she was somewhere cold and alone and hurt, fighting for her life so she could come back to her baby.

RUNNING ON LITTLE TO NO sleep, the next morning John made coffee, then phoned the Butterville Inn. Doris, the owner, answered in her usual cheerful voice.

"Morning, Doris, it's Chief Wise."

"What can I do for you, Chief?"

"I was wondering if you have any strangers who registered at the inn last night or the night before."

"How come?"

He scrubbed a hand over the back of his neck. The

downside of a small town was that everyone knew everyone else's business. Of course, that also worked in his favor sometimes.

"A woman was attacked at Samantha Corley's house night before last. Judging from the prints and blood I found, I believe it was Honey Dawson."

"Honey Dawson, oh my word. Has that little hussy come back to town?"

"Doris," John said tightly. "I believe she's hurt, in trouble, she may even be dead. I'm trying to find her and the man who attacked her."

"Oh, yes, I'm sorry, John. It's just that Honey broke my son Andrew's heart years ago. I thought he'd never get over it."

Honey had broken a lot of hearts. "Just tell me about your guest list."

"Right." He heard the rustling of pages. "I can't think of anyone suspicious, John. I've got four families here now, all seem like nice folks with children. You know they come to town to tour Butterville Babyland General."

He rolled his eyes. "No one traveling alone then?"

"No, not right now. But I'll let you know if someone strange comes in." She paused. "And John, I hope you find Honey. I didn't mean to imply that I wanted to see her harmed."

"I know that," John said. The little woman was as sweet as pie and had arthritis so bad she walked with a cane. No way she could hurt anyone.

But her comment made him wonder if there might be someone else in town who harbored a grudge against Honey. Maybe someone who'd seen her drive back into town or known she was coming and didn't want her back.

Maybe Andrew?

And Sam had mentioned Dwayne Hicks. He needed to speak to both of them.

Sam came down the steps already dressed with the baby in her arms, and he nodded good morning. She offered him a tired smile, but the dark smudges beneath her eyes told him she hadn't slept any better than he had.

Emmie whimpered, and Sam grabbed a bottle from the refrigerator, then juggled the baby while she reached for a pot.

He urged her to sit down, took the pot, filled it half full with water and set the bottle inside. Then he poured her a cup of coffee and handed it to her. Her gaze met his and that tingle of awareness once again rippled through him. The temptation to reach out and soothe her seized him so strongly that he gripped his coffee in both hands.

As soon as the water warmed, he handed the bottle to her, and she tested the temperature on her arm. "Perfect."

Emmie latched onto it immediately, her suckling noises filling the tense silence.

Finally he dragged his gaze away from the homey sight of Sam feeding the child and forced himself back to the job. "I phoned the Butterville Inn, but Doris claims that she hasn't had any male strangers register in the last two days. I want to check the two motels on the outside of town today and talk to Dwayne Hicks, and Andrew Banning."

"Andrew?"

"Doris said Honey broke his heart a while back."

"Andrew wouldn't hurt her." She glanced at the baby. "He moved on and seems happy. He told me once that Honey leaving him was the best thing that happened to him. It made him see DeDe in a new light."

He frowned. "Then let's talk to Dwayne."

"You want me to go with you?" Sam asked.

"There's no way I'm leaving you and Emmie alone until this guy is caught."

An odd look crossed Sam's face, then she stood. "All right. Let me pack the diaper bag." Emmie finished the bottle, and Sam pushed the baby toward him. "Will you hold her while I get ready?"

He gave a clipped nod, although holding the child scared the bejeebies out of him. What if he dropped her?

"For heaven's sake, she's not going to bite you, John," Sam said, rolling her eyes. "Just prop her on your shoulder and pat her back. She needs to burp now that she's eaten."

John juggled the baby and managed to fit her against his chest, awkwardly wrapping the fuzzy pink blanket around her. He patted her back gently, terrified he'd hurt her. But a warmth spread through him as she tugged at his collar with her tiny fist. The little thing weighed next to nothing and felt oddly…sweet against him.

Suddenly, she arched her back and let out a loud belch. He grimaced as half the milk she'd just eaten spewed onto his shoulder.

Damn. "Sam!"

Sam rushed in with the diaper bag on her shoulder. "What's wrong?"

"She's sick," he growled. "Should we take her to the hospital?"

Sam chuckled. "She's fine. Sometimes babies just spit up a little after they eat."

"A little?" He peered at the mess, his stomach turning. "It looks like a gallon."

"Oh, don't be such a wimp," Sam said, then reached

in the bag, pulled out a cloth diaper and dabbed his shirt. "It'll wash out."

He wrinkled his nose. "Yeah, but it stinks."

Her face broke into a full-fledged grin and then she burst into laughter.

"It's not funny, Sam. How am I supposed to question suspects when I smell like…baby throw-up?"

"We'll stop by your place and you can change shirts," she suggested. "Either that or take that one off and I'll use some spot remover."

The idea of undressing in front of Sam seemed appealing, but not with the baby present. "We'll stop by my house."

Sam handed him a photo of Honey. "I thought we might show this picture around."

"Good idea." He jammed the photo in the pocket of his jacket.

It took them twenty more minutes to transfer the car seat into his squad car, then fifteen to stop by his house and for him to change. Emmie had fallen asleep so Sam waited in the car with her until he returned.

First, he drove to the hotel near town known to house tourists during the height of their tourist season. Sam stayed in the car with Emmie while he jogged inside.

The man at the desk regarded him with narrowed eyes as he explained the situation. "Can you check your list and see if any men traveling alone checked in last night or the night before?"

He consulted his listings. "No, don't see any males alone," he said. "Right now we only have a few rooms rented. Five to families, the other five to women traveling with a church group."

John flashed Honey's picture. "How about a woman

who might have been alone? This woman? Her name is Honey Dawson. She used to live around here and could have been hurt."

He tapped his knuckles on the counter. "No, no one like that. I'm sorry, Chief Wise."

John clicked his teeth. "Well, if you see anyone or anything suspicious, please give me a call. If this woman is still alive, she may be in grave danger."

The hotel attendant agreed, and John rushed back outside. "No luck there. Let's try the truck stop near the highway."

Emmie had fallen asleep, and Sam reached back to tuck the blanket more securely around her. They drove in silence to the motel. Again, Sam waited inside the car.

Wind rustled the trees as he walked up to the entrance to the dive. Two eighteen-wheelers were parked in front, the drivers, two beefy men perched at the breakfast bar eating and drinking coffee.

John introduced himself. "Where are you guys heading?"

"I'm on my way to Alabama with a load," the beefier one answered. "Just pulled in this morning for a bite to eat."

"How about you?" John asked the older man.

"I wanted to keep driving, but my wife said we have to stop here. She's determined to buy one of those danged dolls for our little girl."

A rail-thin woman with bleached blond hair rolled in, a cigarette dangling from her mouth. "You damn right I do," she said. "Kristi's been begging for one for two years now, and I'm going to surprise her for her birthday."

John sighed. This was a dead end. Still, he flashed

Honey's picture. No one recognized it, but they all agreed to keep their eyes open.

John strode to the counter and greeted a heavyset woman with red curly hair and bright blue eye shadow. "What can I do for you, Chief?"

He explained about Honey's disappearance and flashed Honey's picture. "Any strangers in here the last two nights?"

"Wow, that girl is a looker." She jammed a pencil in her bird nest hairdo. "I haven't seen her. It's been dead as doornails around here. But it'll pick up in a couple of weeks and we'll be overflowing."

John bit back a remark, knowing the locals depended on the revenue from the upcoming Butterbean doll festival.

"Well, call me if you see her or any strange males show up."

She agreed and he went back outside to Sam.

"Sorry, no luck there." He started the engine. "Let's go talk to Dwayne."

"I just hope he knows something," Sam said as a gust of wind picked up and the skies darkened. "The weatherman is predicting that we're in for bad weather, John. If Honey is alone and hurt in the woods, we need to hurry."

John gritted his teeth. Sam was right. If the temperature dropped, the mountains would be freezing. And that would be dangerous, maybe even deadly, for an injured woman.

SAM STRUGGLED TO BE OPTIMISTIC, but the darkening skies and falling temperatures added to her anxiety. She twisted her hands in her lap as John drove to Dwayne's.

Hopefully he hadn't already left for work, but if so, they could catch him at the garage. He was the best mechanic in town.

She sighed in relief when she spotted his red pickup in the drive.

"I want to go in this time," Sam said.

"All right, but let me ask the questions, Sam."

She reached over and laid her hand on his. "John, maybe I should talk to him. Dwayne might be more willing to open up if he thinks you aren't here to accuse him of something."

He studied her for a long moment but finally conceded with a nod. "But if I think he's lying or holding back, I will come down on him, Sam. I don't care if you guys were friends."

"He wouldn't hurt Honey," Sam said. "I know it. But maybe she contacted him for help, even confided who Emmie's father was."

She climbed out, scooped up the little girl and cradled her in the blanket as they walked up to Dwayne's mobile home.

Sally, Dwayne's wife, answered the door with a scowl. "Sam? Chief Wise? What are you doing here?"

"Sally," Sam said with a tentative smile, "we need to come in and talk to Dwayne."

"Is Dwayne in some kind of trouble?" Sally asked warily.

"No, of course not," Sam said. "But we still need to talk to him."

Sally glanced at the baby with a scowl, but gestured for them to enter, then yelled for Dwayne. He appeared a moment later wearing a gray pair of work coveralls with his name embroidered on the pocket.

"Sam?" he said in surprise, then frowned when he saw John. "Chief Wise, what are you doing here?"

"We came to talk to you about Honey Dawson," Sam said.

A tick jumped in Dwayne's jaw. "What about Honey? Did something happen to her?"

"Why would you ask that?" John asked.

Dwayne jammed his hands in his pockets. "Why else would you be here? Is she all right, Sam? Did something bad happen to her?"

Sam glanced at John, then back at Dwayne. His wife moved up beside him and slid her hand to his arm.

"I don't know, Dwayne. That's why we're here." The baby whimpered, and Sam jiggled her in her arms. "The night before last Honey left this baby at my house. When I got home, there was blood on the floor, but Honey was gone. It looked as if someone dragged her out the back door."

Dwayne paled, and stumbled over to the sofa and sat down. His wife glared at them, then joined him and took his hand. "I'm sure she's okay, Dwayne. You know Honey. She always comes out on top."

Sam cleared her throat. Obviously Dwayne still cared about Honey. "Dwayne, have you heard anything from Honey lately? Did she write you or call you?"

His panicked gaze shot to his wife and guilt riddled his face. "She called a while back, maybe two or three weeks ago."

"What did she say?" John asked.

Dwayne gripped his wife's hand. "Just that she might be coming back to town."

Sally dug her nails into Dwayne's arms. "Dwayne hasn't seen her, Chief."

"I haven't," Dwayne said, his jaw ticking again. "I promised Sally I wouldn't."

John cleared his throat. "How about you, Sally? You obviously didn't want your husband meeting up with an old girlfriend, did you?"

She lurched up, her red-painted lips pressed in a firm line. "I don't like your implication, Chief."

Sam spoke up. "Sally, did you hear from Honey or see her?"

"No," Sally said emphatically as she glanced at the baby again.

"Is that baby Honey's?" Dwayne blurted.

Sam started to answer, but John cut her off. "We don't know," John said. "We're running DNA to find out."

A sour look twisted Sally's thin face. "She probably stole the baby. You know Honey was always trouble."

"Honey would never take a child unless she thought the baby was in danger," Sam said. The realization added another possible avenue for them to explore. She believed the baby was Honey's, but if not, maybe she had discovered the mother or father was abusing the child and wanted to save her.

No. The baby looked too much like Honey not to be hers.

Still, they needed to find Honey to get some answers.

"Where were you both the night before last?" John asked.

Sally stroked Dwayne's arm. "We were here to-gether."

John gave Dwayne a pointed look. "Is that right?"

Dwayne nodded, but his eyes darted away nervously.

Sam studied Dwayne's body language. There was

something he wasn't telling them, something he didn't want to say in front of his wife.

They needed to get him alone.

"Thanks for your time," John said. "And if you think of anything that could help or if you hear from Honey, let me know."

"Of course," Dwayne said.

Sam and John stepped outside, hesitating on the front steps as the sound of Dwayne's and Sally's voices rose in anger.

"Dwayne, did you see Honey?" Sally said in a shrill tone.

"No," Dwayne muttered in a shaky voice, "I promised you I wouldn't."

"What about that baby, Dwayne?" Sally screeched. "Is that baby yours and Honey's?"

Chapter Seven

Sam craned her head to hear Dwayne's response to Sally's question. Had Dwayne met Honey somewhere and hooked up with her again?

Was Emmie Dwayne's child?

"Sally," Dwayne said in an almost patronizing voice, "you know that I would never cheat on you."

"But you still love *her,* you always have," Sally said in disgust. "I don't know what it is about that woman. She's like the Pied Piper except instead of children following behind her, it's men."

"Honey is not a bad person," Dwayne said. "She's really loving. She just can't settle down."

"She's a slut," Sally said viciously. "I bet that blond hair comes out of a bottle."

"She's a natural," Dwayne said, and John shot Sam a look that said Dwayne was an absolute fool for defending Honey and the naturalness of her hair color.

Footsteps pounded, and Sam grimaced and peeked through the window, wondering if their argument might get physical. She didn't think Dwayne would ever hit a woman, but Sally had always been volatile and the jealous type.

"Tell me the truth, Dwayne." Sally pinned him with narrowed eyes. "Is that brat yours?"

Sam flinched at the desperate tone to Sally's voice. If Dwayne answered yes, no telling what Sally would do.

"No, of course not." Dwayne scrubbed his fingers through his hair, spiking it into disarray. "I haven't seen Honey in over a year."

"But you talked to her," Sally accused. "I saw her number on your phone log."

"You snooped on my phone," Dwayne said, his tone appalled. "My God, Sally, you need help."

More footsteps clattered, and Sam and John hurried down the steps toward the car. Sam expected Dwayne to barrel out the front door, but he must have gone toward the back, because they made it to the car without incident.

"What do you think?" John asked.

Sam heaved a breath. "That we need to talk to Dwayne alone. I don't think Emmie is his. Dwayne's not a cheater, but he might know more."

John studied her for a moment. "Wait awhile then call him on his cell. Maybe he knows who the father of the baby is."

Sam grew pensive. Maybe he did. If not, perhaps he could tell them the full name of the guy she'd met in Montgomery, and any other men she might have met after she'd left.

John gestured toward the pickup truck parked next to a green four-door sedan. "Didn't you say that the car that tried to run you down was a dark sedan?"

Sam nodded, a shiver running down her spine. Sally was obviously jealous of Honey. If she'd suspected Emmie was Dwayne's or that he would hook back up with her, would Sally try to kill Honey and her baby?

JOHN'S PHONE BUZZED and he checked the number—
Deputy Floyd. He quickly connected the call while Sam
soothed the baby.

"Have you found anything?" John asked.

"No. We've searched the north hills and located a
couple of abandoned old houses, but there were no
signs that anyone was there."

John pinched the bridge of his nose. "Keep looking.
And organize a group to search behind Sam's house
again, but this time extend the area to a five-mile
radius."

"Will do."

His phone beeped with another call, and he saw it
was his father. His deputy disconnected, and he considered not taking his father's call, but there was no use
putting it off.

"John, what's going on there? I talked to the mayor,
and he said he stopped by your office but you weren't
in. Your deputy told him you might have a murder."

Sam strapped the baby into the car seat and settled
her in the car, but he remained outside, wanting privacy.
"Yes, Dad," he said, then explained about Honey and
the attack on Samantha.

"Don't tell me you're actively pursuing this," his
father said in a brittle tone. "If you have to put someone
else on the investigation to make it look good, do so.
But I want you in Atlanta in two days to meet with the
financial backers I've lined up. They're looking for a gu-
bernatorial candidate and I want your name in the mix."

John gritted his teeth. "Dad, I'll see if I can get this
case resolved by then, but I can't make promises. A
murder here in Butterville is huge and I'm in charge."

"Who cares about that trampy girl?" his father snapped.

"Samantha Corley for one," John said, irritated. His father might hold a senate seat, but he wouldn't tell him how to do his job. "And if Honey, her baby, Sam or any other citizen in this town is in danger, I'm going to damn well do everything I can to protect them."

A long, tense pause stretched between them, his father's anger palpable. "Just don't let this job interfere with the bigger picture, son. You're too smart and have too bright a future to stay in that Podunk town."

His father had told him that for years, but for the first time, John found his father's attitude snobby. "The people in this town may be country," he said between gritted teeth. "But what kind of cop, man or politician would I make if I didn't do my job here, if I decided one person's life was more valuable over another's?" His own anger rose. "Not the kind of man I'd want elected."

His father hissed, but John didn't wait on a response. He disconnected the call.

He wouldn't let his father sway him into leaving town before he found Honey and he knew the baby and Sam were safe.

He'd made Sam a promise and he intended to keep it.

"CAN YOU THINK OF ANYWHERE else Honey might go or someone she might turn to if she had escaped her attacker?" John asked.

"I don't think she kept in touch with anyone else." Sam chewed her lower lip in thought. "But she might turn to Miss Mazie."

John steered the car onto the highway. "Then let's go see Miss Mazie."

Sam contemplated how to get Dwayne alone while John drove the short distance to the older woman's house. A mixture of emotions welled in Sam's chest as they parked and walked up to the two-story antebellum house. It had seen its better days, but she could still see Honey and her and the other kids Miss Mazie had cared for playing in the front yard, swaying in the tire swing hanging from the giant oak, chanting rhymes as they rocked on the wraparound porch.

Sam knocked and John shifted, checking the window as they waited on Miss Mazie to shuffle to the door. She was in her late sixties now and had undergone a knee replacement and relied on a cane, but her short brown curls were void of gray and her eyes were alert as she opened the door.

"Samantha, baby, it's good to see you." The older woman glanced at the baby in Sam's arms with a curious eye raise, then at John, and a wariness crossed her face as if she realized something was wrong. "Hello, John. My, you've gotten to be a big good-looking man."

John shifted uncomfortably, jamming his hands in the pockets of his jeans. "Good to see you, ma'am. It's been a while."

"We need to talk to you," Sam said. "Can we come in?"

"Of course." Miss Mazie gestured for them to enter, and John followed her and Miss Mazie to the kitchen. Miss Mazie set a plate of homemade fried apple pies on the table and poured them a glass of sweet iced tea before sitting down. You couldn't visit Miss Mazie without eating something. Affection for the woman who'd taken her in warmed her as she bit into the juicy apple filling. Miss Mazie had taught her everything she knew about cooking.

Miss Mazie leaned across the table and patted the baby. "Who is this little angel?"

"That's one reason we're here," Sam said.

Miss Mazie's smile faded. "You know, darling, that I don't take children in anymore. I can't, not for more than a night or two."

"I know." Sympathy and affection for Miss Mazie warmed Sam's heart. "And I didn't come to ask you to. It's about Honey."

Alarm flickered in Miss Mazie's gray eyes. "What about my girl Honey?"

Sam explained about finding the baby, the blood on the floor, and that they thought the baby belonged to Honey, omitting John's theory that Honey might have kidnapped the child.

John cast her a curious look, but she refused to let him sully Honey's name in front of Miss Mazie. Apparently he understood her silent warning, that or he realized Miss Mazie would jump down his throat if he started spouting bad things about Honey.

"Have you heard from Honey lately?" Sam asked.

Miss Mazie shook her head and stroked the baby's cheek with gnarled fingers. "No, not in months. The last postcard I received from her was from Dallas. She was excited about trying out for the Dallas Cowboy cheerleaders." A soft sigh escaped her. "Honey always dreamed about that."

Sam nodded. "Well, thanks for your time, Miss Mazie. If you hear from her, please call me."

Miss Mazie clutched Sam's hand as she started to stand, then turned an imploring look toward John. "Please find her, Chief. I don't want that baby to grow up without her mama."

John nodded, and Sam squeezed the woman's hand. "Try not to worry. Honey is a fighter, I know she's out there doing everything she can to get back to her daughter." She hugged Miss Mazie, and Miss Mazie bent to kiss Emmie's forehead. "We'll find her and make sure she raises Emmie. And when they're back together, we'll come to see you."

"I'll start a Butterbean doll for my grandbaby," Miss Mazie said with a sparkle back in her eyes.

John gave Sam an odd look as they headed back outside.

She only hoped that she hadn't just lied to the woman who'd raised her and that they found Honey alive.

Her cell phone rang, and Sam dug inside her purse. "It's Dwayne."

"Answer it," John said.

She clicked to connect the call. "Hey, Dwayne, it's Sam."

"Sam," Dwayne said in a panicked voice. "I want to help you look for Honey."

"Dwayne, I understand it was hard to talk in front of Sally. Do you know something you're not telling me?"

A hesitant pause. "No, not really. But if you have a search party out looking, I'll be glad to help."

"Be honest with me, Dwayne. Did you see Honey when she got to town?"

"No, I swear, I didn't."

"I understand this is hard, Dwayne, but could this baby possibly be yours?"

"No," Dwayne said quickly. "I was telling the truth about that. It's been over a year since I saw Honey."

"How about Sally? Could she have talked to her or seen her?"

Another pause. "I don't know. She's irrational when it comes to Honey. I've told her over and over that there's nothing between me and Honey except friendship, but she swears there's more."

"Do you think she would hurt Honey?"

Dwayne hissed a breath. "I don't want to believe that she would."

Sam's stomach knotted. Not wanting to believe wasn't the same as believing. "But you're not sure?"

"She was with me night before last," he said, but his voice cracked.

Sam sighed. "Did Honey tell you she had a baby?"

"No. I wish she'd admitted she was in trouble. She knows I would have helped her."

Sam's heart clenched for him. She could almost understand Sally's jealousy. Honey had that kind of effect on men. They couldn't help but fall all over her. "Dwayne, if you're not Emmie's father, then we need to find out who is. Do you have any idea?"

"I don't know. Maybe you should ask that guy Randy she met in Montgomery."

Emmie began to fuss, and Sam glanced at John. She was probably getting hungry again. "We'd like to, Dwayne. Do you know his last name?"

"Ackerman," Dwayne said. "He worked at Billy Bob's Barbeque with Honey."

"Thanks, Dwayne," Sam said. "We'll see if we can find him. Maybe he can give us more information."

"What did he say?" John asked when she closed her phone.

"That he's not Emmie's father, but we should talk to Randy Ackerman, the guy she left him for."

"Do you think he was telling the truth?"

"About seeing Honey—yes." Sam twisted her hands together. "But Sally is the one who worries me."

What if her irrational jealousy had turned violent?

"SALLY IS SUSPICIOUS," John said. "But that partial footprint seemed too large for a woman." He maneuvered the car around the curve. "Of course Sally could have hired help. Does she have a brother or someone in town who might do something illegal for her?"

"Not that I know of."

"Let's go by the station and I'll see what can dig up on Randy Ackerman."

The baby whimpered from the back, and Sam turned to try to comfort her. "We'll stop soon and I'll feed you, sweetie pie. It won't be long, I promise."

John's cell phone buzzed, and he checked the number. It was his deputy so he quickly connected the call. "Chief Wise."

"Chief, I don't know if this has anything to do with Honey Dawson, but we found footprints and blood by the river near the old mill. We also found a locket."

"I'll be right there." He disconnected the call, turned the car around on a side road and headed toward the river.

"What is it?" Sam asked. "Did they find Honey?"

"No, but my deputy found blood and footprints down by the river."

Fear clouded Sam's eyes, and she gazed out the window as he wound his way to the old mill. The SUV bounced over the ruts in the road, the baby's cries escalating, adding to the tension. Gigantic trees created a canopy along the highway, the mountain stream gurgling along the road.

John scrubbed his hand over the back of his neck,

sweating. The crisp fall wind rattled the leaves, sending them raining down as he parked and climbed out.

"John, do you mind getting a bottle from that bag?" Sam asked as she hurried to scoop up the baby. Emmie was crying ferociously now, and he dug for the bottle, rushed around to her side of the car and handed it to her. She cradled the little girl in her arms and the baby instantly quieted as she latched on to eat.

The deputy was crouched down beside a patch of weeds by the river, and Sam followed John to the edge to speak to him. Blood dotted the pile of rocks, and partial footprints marred the mud, although John doubted they would be enough to get a match.

Deputy Floyd looked up at him, a delicate silver chain with a heart locket attached dangling from his fingers. "I found this necklace by the rocks. Could belong to the missing girl."

"Or anyone else who'd been hiking or camping here lately," John muttered, although the blood did look suspicious.

Sam made a strangled sound behind him, then stepped forward and touched the locket. "This is Honey's." She traced a finger over the etching on the front. "It was the only thing her mother left with her when she abandoned her."

She glanced at the river raging over the jagged rocks, and a tortured expression darkened her eyes

Sympathy welled in John's chest. He placed his hand on the small of her back to comfort her, the silence stretching between them as the implications set in.

What if the man had killed Honey and dumped her body in the river?

Chapter Eight

Memories flooded Sam as she stared at the silver locket. Honey had laughed in a sad sort of way when she'd told Sam about her mother's parting gift. The locket wasn't expensive, but the word Love was etched on the back. Honey had insisted that etching meant that her mother had loved her in spite of the fact that she'd left her on the doorstep of a church in the middle of the night.

But even though she'd left the locket with Honey, there hadn't been any pictures inside—none of her mother or father or even of Honey. It had been empty.

Sam gritted her teeth. She had thought that gift the cruelest of all and had decided that Honey's mother had had an empty heart like that locket.

John stroked her back, and she blinked back tears as she rocked the baby in her arms and stared at the river. The current was strong, the fall wind whipping dry leaves around her feet, the temperature in the mountains dropping with the hint of bad weather.

The river in the mountains never got truly warm, and this time of year it was icy.

Couple that with the fact that Honey had obviously been injured, and bleeding, that she didn't weigh much more than a hundred pounds, that Honey had never learned to swim and that if someone had overpowered her and thrown her in the river, and she might not have survived.

A tear trickled from her eye, and she lifted one hand to swipe at it.

No! Panic screamed through Sam's head. Honey was not dead. Not her best friend.

She refused to believe it.

She would know if Honey was gone; she'd feel it.

"Sam?" John said. "You're sure this was Honey's necklace?"

She swallowed hard and pulled herself together. "Yes. Honey never took it off."

His gaze met hers, concern glittering in his eyes. "I'm sorry."

Anger rolled through her. "She's not dead, John. She's not."

Emmie finished the bottle, and Sam lifted the baby to her shoulder and patted her back.

"Sam, I know you want to believe that, but you have to face the truth, that it's possible that she didn't survive."

"I don't have to face anything yet," Sam said. "Honey is a survivor. I won't believe that she's gone, not unless you show me her body."

John frowned. "I'm sorry, Sam. I really am."

"Don't be sorry," Sam snapped. "Just find her, John."

He stared at her for a long moment, then nodded, turned to his deputy and spoke in a commanding voice. "Let's get a team out here to drag the river."

Sam swayed slightly, his words suggesting a harsh reality that she didn't want to face. Honey was the only person she'd ever been close to.

If her best friend was gone, then she was all alone.

The baby swatted her tiny fingers at Sam's shoulder and her heart lurched. No, she wasn't alone. She had Honey's little girl, and she would raise her as her own.

And Emmie would know that her mother hadn't abandoned her, that she'd loved her with all her heart.

With a gloved hand John took the necklace. "I'll have this checked for fingerprints." He flipped open the locket and Sam peered inside, her heart thumping. The locket had always been empty, but now there was a picture of Emmie on one side.

"Oh, my God," she whispered. There was another photo on the opposite side. A picture of a second baby, this one wrapped in a pale blue blanket.

"They're twins," Sam said in shock.

John met her gaze. "Yeah. But where is the baby boy?"

The crew arrived to drag the river and search the woods, and Sam closed her eyes.

Please don't let Honey and her little boy be dead.

JOHN'S HEAD POUNDED with questions. The locket certainly suggested that Emmie and her twin were Honey's babies. So where was the little boy? Had he been with Honey when she'd arrived in town?

"John," Sam said in a shaky voice. "What if—"

"Shh," he said, and pulled her up next to him. "Don't assume anything. There was only one car seat in Honey's car. Maybe she left the baby boy with someone else."

"But why wouldn't she have brought them both to me?"

"I don't know," John said, his own mind racing with various scenarios. One, that they had been right and whoever had hurt Honey and tried to run Sam off the road wanted the baby. Maybe both of them. "Maybe Honey thought that she could keep them safer if they were apart, so she left the little boy with another friend."

Sam exhaled, obviously trying to regain her composure. "That makes sense. If so, then maybe the little boy is safe."

He had no idea, but he didn't want to panic Sam any more than she already was. "Hopefully so. We just have to figure out who she left the baby with. Maybe that person has answers about who is after Honey and the babies."

Sam seemed to gather her iron-clad control around her, and obviously held on to her hope.

John squeezed her shoulder. "I need to talk to my deputy and coordinate the search. Will you be okay?"

She lifted her stubborn chin although worry still strained her features. "Of course. Go talk to them. Maybe Honey escaped here at the river, and she's in those woods hiding out."

"Could be," he said, although he doubted it. More likely that she had been dumped in that river and that they'd find her body.

Although the current could have swept her downstream, miles and miles away.

The wind picked up and Sam shivered.

"Take the baby to the car and wait," John said softly. "This is going to take some time."

Sam glanced at the river and then him, but hugged Emmie to her, tightening the blanket around the little girl's shoulders as she walked away. He gritted his teeth and strode over to meet his deputy.

Who in the hell would want to hurt that little baby, and why?

WHAT A NIGHTMARE.

Sam climbed in the front seat and rocked Emmie back to sleep as she watched a CSI team string crime scene tape around the area and search for forensics. Another team began to drag the river, and others dispersed through the wooded area to search for her friend. One grueling hour bled into another, dark clouds gathering above and threatening rain as evening approached.

News of the search must have spread through town and chaos descended. Men and women showed up to help, many who'd known Honey from high school. No one seemed surprised that Honey had landed in trouble, but all seemed eager to find her.

Dwayne raced up and joined the team in the woods, Sally behind him, her arms crossed as she watched her husband's frantic efforts. Bernice from the local diner arrived, armed with hot coffee and sandwiches.

Sam accepted coffee but declined the food. "Thanks, Bernice, but my stomach is churning. I don't think I could keep down anything right now."

The plump woman patted Sam's shoulder. "I know, sweet, but don't give up. Our Honey is a fighter."

Sam nodded, and glanced at the baby. Honey had two babies now, two reasons to fight for her life. She only hoped it was enough.

Renee Renfree, the reporter from the local paper and one of Honey's co-cheerleaders in high school, arrived and made a dive for Sam. "What can you tell us about Honey's disappearance?"

Sam cleared her throat. "I really don't know much. Just that she's missing."

Renee pointed to Emmie, tucked in Sam's arms. "Is

it true that she was attacked at your home and that she left that baby with you?"

Sam hesitated, and John suddenly appeared by the car and shoved away the microphone. "This is an official investigation, Renee. Sam has no comment."

"John," Sam said.

He gave her a sharp look. "No, Sam. Stay out of it."

"Then, Chief, can you tell us what's going on?" Renee shoved the microphone toward John. "Is the baby Honey's? Do you think Honey is dead?"

A muscle throbbed in John's jaw as he reined in his temper. "As you know, we believe Honey Dawson is missing. She may be injured, and she's in danger. If anyone has information about her, please contact the police immediately."

"Is it true that she left a baby—"

John placed his hand over the microphone. "That's it, Renee. This interview is over."

Renee glared at him, but obviously decided she wasn't going to pry any information out of him and moved on to question some of the locals. Sam could only imagine the comments. The men all loved Honey. The women wouldn't be so kind; they'd probably paint her friend as a blatant whore.

Another hour passed, then another, and the clouds opened up and it began to rain. The search teams slowly made their way back in, their expressions grave.

As the rain began to pour down, most of the locals who'd gathered ran to their cars, and John strode toward her, then climbed into the driver's side, swiping damp hair from his eyes.

"Did they find anything?" Sam asked.

"Forensics found a couple of stray blond hairs and

collected them. But so far, nothing in the woods or the river."

Sam pressed a hand to his arm. "That's good news then. It means Honey may still be alive."

He cut his dark eyes toward her. "Sam—"

"I'm not giving up," she said.

His dismal expression offered no hope, and her heart twisted.

"Either way," he said, "we need to trace Honey's movements and find out who was after her and the babies."

Sam glanced back at the baby. Yes. They had to find Honey's little boy and make sure he was safe.

The babies were siblings, twins—they needed to be together.

RAIN POUNDED THE ROOF of his SUV and slashed the windshield as John drove back to Sam's. He wanted to be optimistic for her sake, but the fact that they hadn't found Honey didn't bode well with him. Every day that passed decreased their chances of her being alive.

Her body could have floated downstream, and if she was running for her life in the mountains and injured, she might not survive.

"Are you hungry?" he asked as they drove through town.

"Not really," Sam said.

He gritted his teeth. "Did you eat anything since this afternoon?"

Sam shook her head, twisting her hands together. "I couldn't."

John swung the SUV into the parking lot of the diner. "How about the special of the day?"

"That's fine," Sam said, although he sensed that she was only agreeing to appease him.

John jumped out and slogged through the rain to the door, then stepped inside, shaking rain from his head. The weather must have kept people home because the cozy diner was nearly empty. The scent of turkey and dressing suffused him, and his stomach growled.

"I figured you'd be by tonight," Tonya, the waitress, said with a flirty smile.

He ignored the flirting part. "I need a couple of the specials to go."

"No luck finding Honey?" she asked.

He shook his head. "No, but I'll keep looking."

She packed the food in take-out containers, then added a couple of pieces of homemade cake to the order, and he paid, then rushed back outside. The baby was fussing, so he remained silent until they arrived at Sam's. He grabbed an umbrella from the back and covered her and the child, then guided them inside and returned for the food.

A noise sounded from the bushes, and he jerked his head to the left. The bushes rustled and twigs snapped, the whisk of movement making him tense.

He removed his gun from inside his jacket, wielding it at the ready as he inched around the side of the house. Another sound echoed from the woods beyond and a coyote howled from a nearby ridge.

His chest tightened as he searched the shadows and circled the house, but he didn't find anyone lurking around.

Had he imagined it or had someone been there?

Thunder clapped above, lightning zigzagging across the dark sky and another noise sounded from the front of the house. He ducked in the rain, inching back around and searched for the origin, but saw nothing.

The door swung open, and Sam stood in the doorway. "John?"

"I'm right here," he said as he slid through the shadows and climbed the steps.

"Is something wrong?" she asked.

"I just wanted to check the outside," he said. But he remained alert as they went inside the house. Someone was stalking Sam. Someone who wanted the baby.

He'd kill the son of a bitch before he let him hurt either one of them.

HE SLIPPED INTO THE SHADOWS and the safety of the woods and slithered back to his car where he'd parked on the dirt road that led to those old chicken houses. Grateful to be out of the rain, he checked his messages and punched in a return call.

"It's me."

"Did you take care of that kid yet?"

He clenched the phone with one hand while swiping rain from his face and neck with a handkerchief. "No. This local cop is all over the woman Honey left the brat with."

"You need to do it soon before he figures out what's going on."

"I know that. How about the other baby?"

"I have a lead and I'm closing in. You take care of your end and let me worry about this one."

"How about Honey?"

He hesitated, sweat beading on his forehead. "Taken care of."

"Good. Now finish up and make sure you don't leave a trail behind you."

He disconnected the call, then sat and stared into the canopy of trees for hours, until the rain finally dwindled. Determined, he climbed out, pulled on fireproof gloves, then grabbed matches and the old rags he'd tied together in the trunk. Adrenaline churned through him as he doused them with kerosene.

Pulling his coat around his neck to ward off the chill, he walked back through the woods to the Corley woman's house, his boots sinking into the mud. Darkness bathed the exterior of the house, and barring a light from the kitchen, the inside lights were off.

He struck the match, lit the end of the cloth and tossed it onto the front porch beneath the door where the wood flooring and door were dry. Flames flickered upward, the fire catching along the edges of the door. He tossed another below the window. Then he crept around to the side of the house and lit another one and tossed it against the back door beneath the awning.

A smile curved his mouth as he watched the flames catch. Soon the house would be on fire. Then that damn baby and the Corley woman would be toast, and his problems would be over.

Chapter Nine

John jerked awake from the den chair where he'd kept vigil over Sam and the baby. He'd had a feeling the stalker had been watching, biding his time until he could strike.

The scent of smoke wafted through the cracks and seeped into the room, and he jumped up, instantly alert. They hadn't lit a fire in the fireplace.

He blinked to focus, then hesitated, trying to detect the source of the smell. The front of the house? The back?

He ran to the kitchen door. Smoke seeped through the bottom of the door, choking the air. He hurried to the front and saw flames crackling along the seams of the door, smoke beginning to flow through the foyer. A quick check through the window, and he spotted flames shooting upward along the door and along the floor beneath the front windows.

Dammit, the bastard had lit them up on both sides. He wanted to rush outside and catch him. He was probably hanging around to watch.

But Sam and the baby were in danger, and they came first.

He stabbed the numbers for the fire department. "Get

out to Samantha Corley's right now. Someone set the place on fire."

He hung up, ran upstairs and vaulted into Sam's room. She lay sleeping on her side, tucked beneath a homemade quilt. He knew she was exhausted and hadn't slept or rested since the night Honey had shown up in her house, and he hated to wake her, but he had to.

He leaned over and shook her gently. "Sam?"

At that moment, the smoke detector finally went off with a shrill beep. Sam jerked awake and stared up at him, sleep and confusion clouding her eyes.

"Sam," he said in the calmest voice he could muster. "Someone set the house on fire outside. I've called the fire department, but you need to get up."

Panic flashed in her eyes for only a brief second before she threw the covers off her and reached for a robe and shoes. He shoved the robe into her hands. "Get the baby. I'll try to contain the blaze until the fire department arrives."

She nodded, her eyes wide, but dragged on the robe, stuffed her feet into the shoes and followed him as he ran from the room.

"Do you have a fire extinguisher?" he asked as they raced into the hall.

She gave a terror-stricken nod. "Yes, one upstairs and one in the kitchen."

"Get the one up here and use it to protect you and Emmie if you need it. I'll take the downstairs and try to stop the flames from spreading inside."

They parted at the door to her bedroom, and she ran to get the baby while he raced downstairs and grabbed the fire extinguisher.

The flames were licking along the front door and windows as he peered out, and he dared not open the door, so he knocked out the window in the laundry room off the kitchen and climbed through it. He dropped to the ground and hurried to the back of the house. The fire was small on the stoop but eating at the wood, and he sprayed the fire extinguisher to douse the flames. Precious minutes passed, his nerves on edge. With the rain dwindling, how fast would the front porch catch and the smoke curl inside?

But as soon as he extinguished the back doorway, he raced back inside. Sam had gathered Emmie and was in the den, crouched down low, covering the baby's mouth and nose to prevent her from inhaling the smoke. He grabbed the fire extinguisher from her, then coaxed her toward the kitchen.

"Come on, let's go out back."

She nodded and ran beside him, clutching the baby to her in a death grip as they raced onto the lawn and around to the front.

"Wait here with Emmie," he yelled, then he ran toward the front porch. Flames were inching up the railing all along the front door and spreading on the porch.

He aimed the fire extinguisher and sprayed the flames, hoping like hell that now Sam and Emmie were safe, that he could save her house.

SAM WATCHED IN HORROR as the fire engine roared up her drive and screeched to a halt. The siren's wail burst into the night and woke the baby, and she began to scream. Sam jiggled her up and down to calm her, her own heart racing.

"Shh, precious, it's all right." She nuzzled Emmie's cheek with her own. "You're safe now. I won't let anything bad happen to you. I promise."

Smoke curled upward into the sky, blackening the white painted wood and porch, the flames licking toward her wicker furniture.

Shock set in, mingling with raw anger as Sam's adrenaline waned. She couldn't believe that someone had tried to burn them out of her home. Someone who could have killed not only her and John but a sweet, little innocent girl who'd never hurt anyone in her life.

The pure injustice of it reminded her of her past and the stories she heard on the job, and rage replaced her fear. "We'll find out who did this, Emmie, and make them pay."

A team of firefighters jumped from the truck and began to roll the hose toward the house. John met one of them on the porch and turned the task over to them while he pulled his gun and began to circle the house in case the arsonist was lurking around.

Fear made her chest clench as John disappeared into the woods. Had John seen her stalker in the trees? Had the man set fire to the house, then stood by and watched to see if they'd died?

One of the firemen approached her carrying a blanket and wrapped it around her. "Ma'am, are you and the baby all right?"

"Yes," she said through a thick throat.

He leaned around her to examine the baby. "Are you sure? Do either one of you need a doctor? Did the little one inhale smoke?"

"No, we got out in time," she said. Thanks to John and his quick thinking.

"Can you tell me what happened? Do you know how the fire got started?"

She shivered, swaying back and forth gently to rock Emmie. "We were asleep, and someone must have set it outside."

His sandy-haired brow shot up. "You think it was arson?"

"Yes," she said, her teeth gritted. "Chief Wise was at my house because someone has been stalking me, someone who wants to hurt this baby."

His young face looked shocked but resigned. "I see. I'll tell the fire inspector to search for an accelerant and trace evidence."

With a quick adjustment to his fire hat, he strode over to consult with the other firefighters. She paced back and forth, continuing to soothe Emmie as she watched the flames slowly die and the smoke waft upward and fade into a hazy cloud.

Minutes ticked by, rolling into an hour. The firefighters finally extinguished the last of the waning flames. Thankfully they'd managed to contain the fire to the front porch, but the scent of the charred wood filled the air, the black ashes and soot reminding her of how close she and Honey's daughter had come to dying.

An inspector arrived to sift through the debris, and she continued to pace, hugging Emmie to her as she searched the thicket of trees surrounding her property for John.

A gunshot suddenly blasted the air, and she froze, her heart constricting. Had John fired his gun, or had the man who'd set the fire shot at him?

JOHN SPOTTED A SILHOUETTE of a man running through the woods and chased him through the trees. The man turned and fired at him, and John ducked behind an oak and fired back.

The bullet pinged an evergreen beside him, but the man skidded down the embankment, sending rocks skittering. John vaulted forward to follow him. By the time he made it to the top of the embankment, the sound of a car engine roared to life. He jogged down the hill, sliding as his feet skidded on the wet pine straw and the car raced away.

Dammit.

He pushed to his feet and fired through the clearing, then chased after the car and fired again, trying to get a read on the license plate, but it was too far away. His breath rushed out as he jogged faster but the car accelerated, tires squealing, slinging gravel at him as it disappeared around the curve.

He cursed again and lowered his weapon. There was no way in hell he could catch the guy on foot, and by the time he raced back to his car, the vehicle would be miles away.

Furious, he turned and climbed back up the hill, then wove through the woods toward Sam's. By the time he reached the clearing and her house, the thick smoke was diminishing, and the firefighters had gotten the situation under control. The acrid scent of the charred wood still filled the air though, and he spotted Sam pacing with the baby in the driveway near the fire engine.

The first strains of morning bled through the sky as the sun fought its way through the storm clouds. Sam suddenly pivoted, saw him and ran toward him, hugging the baby to her.

Relief softened the fear in her eyes, and she flew at

him. "John, my God, I heard the shots and thought you might be hurt."

His gut tightened, and he reached out and pulled her closer to him. "No, I'm fine. I chased him through the woods, but he escaped."

A frown marred her face. "So he was watching?"

"I'm afraid so." He stroked her arm, the image of what could have happened tonight taunting him. "Sam, I want you and Emmie in a safe house until we find this guy."

"No," Sam said. "I'm not running. I want to find Honey."

"Listen to me," he said, then pressed a hand to her cheek. "This guy has tried to kill you more than once. I want you safe so I can investigate."

She cut her eyes toward the house where the evidence of just how dangerous the situation was dared her to argue. With a shaky breath, she trailed her finger along the baby's soft blond curls. "No, we'll take Emmie someplace safe. Then I'm going to help you find Honey."

He studied her for a long tension-filled moment. "Where would you put the baby? With Miss Mazie?"

She sighed, distress heavy in the sound. "Only if you can put a guard on her. I don't want this guy to track her there and hurt Miss Mazie."

"That I can do," he said. "We'll pull a fake, leave the baby with Miss Mazie and a guard, and make this guy think we still have her. Then if he comes after us, we'll be ready."

The fire inspector approached them, and John pulled away from her and shook the man's hand. "Dave, thanks for coming out. What did you find?"

The gray-haired man frowned. "Definite signs of arson. It looks like the perp doused some old rags in kerosene, then lit them against the porch. We'll collect what forensics we can and take it to the lab."

"Thanks."

The firefighters rolled up the hose and gathered their equipment, and John and Sam walked back up to the house. "There's probably water damage now," John said. "You'll have to contact your insurance company."

"I'm not worried about the house," Sam said. "I just want to stop this guy and find Honey."

"Let's go in, shower and pack a bag. Then we'll talk to Miss Mazie and contact the guy Honey met up with in Alabama."

He led her around to the back door and they went inside. When Sam saw the water damage in the foyer, her face clouded with anguish. John silently vowed to make it up to her, and to see a smile on her face before he left Butterville.

SAM TUCKED EMMIE BACK into the portable crib and covered her up, then hurried to the shower. Hopefully the baby would be safe at Miss Mazie's so she and John could figure out what was going on and find Honey and her little boy.

She undressed, stepped into the shower, then scrubbed her body and hair, hoping to alleviate the scent of smoke clinging to her skin. Her nerves pinged back and forth as she replayed the evening and the fire.

And that gunshot—for a moment she'd imagined John bleeding and dying in the woods, all because he'd rushed into the dark to protect her and Honey's daughter. Emotions had nearly overwhelmed her. But she'd maintained her control in front of the firemen and John.

But alone in the shower, the pent-up emotions raged to the surface, and she allowed the tears to fall. Her body shook with sobs, and she leaned against the shower wall and breathed deeply as the warm water sluiced over her, soothing away the aches from lack of sleep and the anxiety riddling her.

She didn't know how long she stood there, purging her emotions, but the water began to get cold and eventually she calmed, flipped off the water and climbed from the shower. Chilled, she dried off quickly, then pulled on her thick terry cloth robe, combed through her wet hair and blew it dry, letting the long strands fall around her shoulders. Knowing that John was probably waiting on her downstairs, she stepped into her bedroom, but the door to the hall was open, and John stood inside the doorway, a feral expression on his face.

"What's wrong?" Panic stabbed her. "Did something happen? Did you hear news about Honey?"

"No, Sam, no news." He stared at her for a long moment, his hands fisted beside him, his expression tortured. "Are you all right?"

She nodded, although inside she felt as if she were wilting, as if she might crumble again any minute. She didn't like that feeling and folded her arms, then turned away. She dealt with emotional situations and traumatic family relationships in a professional capacity, but none of them hit as close to home as this one.

"Sam…"

She closed her eyes, battling more emotions, then suddenly felt John move up behind her. He gently gripped her arms and turned her around to face him. She sighed shakily, and stiffened, but he made a guttural noise deep in his throat.

"God, Sam…"

Her gaze swung up to his, and the intensity in his dark eyes sucker punched her. A strength and powerful protectiveness radiated from him as he enveloped her in his arms.

Sam leaned into him, her heart stuttering. His heat felt heavenly, his touch wonderful, soothing, titillating against her shivering body, his scent erotic and so enticing that when he lifted her chin with his thumb and caressed her jaw, she parted her lips, closed her eyes and imagined kissing him.

A second later, his lips touched hers, and he slid his hands to her waist and pulled her up against him as he claimed her mouth with his.

Chapter Ten

John pressed his lips over Sam's, tasting her stubborn sweetness as he pulled her firmly against him. Her plump breasts teased his chest, her hips flaring enticingly beneath his hands as his hard length brushed her abdomen.

A soft purr of desire sounded from her throat, spiking his hunger, and he deepened the kiss, probing her mouth with his tongue. She parted her lips and welcomed him inside with another purr that sent his pulse racing. He wanted to strip that damn robe and feel her bare skin beneath his fingers. A surge of longing ripped through him, and he stroked her waist through the robe, sliding his hand down against her hip to press her more firmly against his sex.

She moved subtly against him as if she felt his arousal and liked it, and he clutched her tighter, brushing his tongue along her lips, then dropping a kiss on her ear and lower to her neck.

Her freshly bathed skin tasted like strawberries, exotic woman and stubbornness, all the wonderful things that made Sam so special. He suckled her neck gently, and she threaded her fingers in his hair pulling him closer and angling her neck to offer him better access. Desire and hunger heated his blood.

Sam could have died tonight in that fire, and he might never have tasted or touched her. Somehow that felt wrong, as if it would have been a terrible loss, but he didn't stop to analyze the reason.

He only knew that at this moment, he wanted her desperately. Wanted to make them both feel alive. Wanted to erase her fears and sadness and replace those emotions with joy and excitement.

Wanted to feel her writhing beneath him, giving herself to him, twining her body with his.

His lips trailed lower, licking, suckling, nibbling at her bare skin, and her chest rose with a sharp intake of breath. Driven to please her, his fingers found the lapel of her robe and he parted the top just enough to dive deeper with his mouth. She moaned softly, slid her foot against his calf and stroked his leg, torturing him.

He nibbled at the upper curve of her breasts, his mouth watering to taste her, his sex hardening and aching. A fierce, primal need ripped through him, and he imagined throwing her on the floor and pounding himself inside her.

The realization jerked him back to reality.

This was Sam Corley. Tough, tenacious, stubborn Sam who had a baby in the next room, a baby she might very well be adopting if they didn't find Honey alive. Sam who would want to stay settled in Butterville.

A place he desperately wanted to leave.

Sam whispered his name, the sound so intimate and sultry that he was tempted to forget any reservations.

But Sam was one woman he wouldn't want to lead on. She wasn't a one-night stand. She needed—and she *deserved*—promises and love and the whole nine yards.

If he made love to her and left, he would hurt her.

Summoning every ounce of restraint and honor he possessed, he slowly pulled away, then tugged the edges of her robe back together and released her. She looked up at him, wild-eyed and aroused, strains of hunger and need brimming in her eyes. That look tore at him and almost made him drag her into his arms and finish what they'd started.

But he liked Sam too much to take advantage of her.

So he took a step back. "I'm sorry, Sam. I got carried away."

Her sultry look sharpened at his apology, and she started to speak, but he held up a warning hand. "It won't happen again. Now get dressed and let's take the baby to Miss Mazie's. Then we're going to find out what happened to Honey and her little boy."

SAM TRIED NOT TO LET JOHN'S dismissal of what had happened between them hurt, but as she rushed to change and he left the room, she wondered if she had done something wrong. She was so damn inexperienced that maybe she'd acted too needy and desperate.

For just a moment, she'd felt a deep connection with him as if he'd wanted her as much as she'd wanted him.

But wanting and needing a man was dangerous. Hadn't she learned a long time ago to stand on her own? Besides, how could she even think of sex now when Honey was missing?

Guilt plagued her and she threw on jeans and a white button shirt, grabbed a sweater and pulled it on, then slipped into the spare room where Emmie was sleeping and packed some of her clothes, diapers, toys, anything Miss Mazie might need. Although the older woman no longer officially took in foster children, she knew Miss Mazie wouldn't turn her down, that she'd take care of Emmie temporarily. She'd do anything she could to help Honey. And Honey's baby was practically her grandchild.

Five minutes later, Sam carried the bag back down the steps. The scent of burned wood and smoke filled the downstairs, reminding her of the earlier attack, and anger and determination set in.

John met her at the steps, his jaw tight. "I'll stow that in the car if you want to get the baby. I talked to Deputy Floyd and he's going to watch Miss Mazie's."

"Good." Sam sighed. "The last thing I want is to put Miss Mazie in danger."

He took the diaper bag from her, and she rushed back up the steps and scooped up Emmie. The baby stirred, but Sam snuggled her closer and Emmie fell back asleep. John met her at the bottom of the steps and walked her to his car, his body tense and alert as he scanned the property.

"I called and made arrangements with Bo Simmons to repair your place."

Sam stiffened. "John, you don't need to do that. I'm perfectly capable of handling my own business."

He frowned as they settled inside. "I know you are, Sam. I was just trying to help. Can't you just say thank you for once?"

She started to argue, but the tension rising between them stemmed from the situation and their earlier encounter. A kiss she wanted to remember—and forget at the same time.

So she sucked up her pride, thanked him, then angled herself to look out the window until they arrived at Miss

Mazie's. John grabbed the diaper bag, and she carried Emmie up to the door. Miss Mazie greeted them with a smile and, as she expected, agreed without question to take care of the baby.

Using their fake-off plan in case the man after them was watching, Sam wrapped one of Miss Mazie's dolls in a baby blanket, cradled it to her as if she were carrying Emmie as they walked to the car. She even made a production of placing it in the car seat and strapping the doll in before climbing in the front seat.

Ten minutes later, they arrived at the police station. John handed her a cup of coffee, and she took the chair by his desk, her anxiety rising while he made a call to the police in Alabama.

When he hung up, he punched in the number for Randy Ackerman. She held her breath, praying that Randy had a lead for them. The storms were threatening again outside, more bad weather approaching.

JOHN PUNCHED IN ACKERMAN'S phone number, determined to stick to business now, solve this case and get the hell out of town before Sam got under his skin any more than she already had.

He tried Ackerman's home phone first, but the man didn't answer, so he punched in his work number next. Ackerman worked at a local food mart and it took a few minutes for the clerk who answered to get him on the line.

"This is Randy, what can I do for you?"

"Mr. Ackerman, this is Chief of Police John Wise from Georgia. I'm calling in reference to a woman named Honey Dawson."

"What about Honey?" the man asked in a breathy voice.

"She's missing and may be hurt."

"What? Oh God…."

The man sounded sincerely worried. "I understand that you and Honey were involved."

"Yeah, but that was months and months ago. I haven't seen Honey in over a year."

John pulled a hand down his face. "What happened between you?"

"Honey was ready to move on," Randy said. "She made it clear from the beginning that she was only stopping through town and wouldn't stay."

"And you were okay with that?" John asked.

A small snort. "Well, yeah. Have you ever met Honey?"

"Yes."

"Then you know she's not the settle-down type. But she can sure make a man feel good. I mean, with a babe like her, a guy takes what he can get."

"So you were okay with her leaving you behind?"

A small hesitation. "What are you getting at, Chief? You think I did something to Honey?"

"I didn't say that, Mr. Ackerman. I'm just trying to locate her, that's all."

The man cleared his throat. "Listen, I had a fling with Honey while she was here, but there were no hard feelings when she left. She wanted to make the Dallas Cowboy cheerleaders and I wanted that for her. Besides, I got another girl now. We're getting married."

Frustration knotted John's neck. "Did you keep in contact with her after she left? Do you know if she got involved with anyone else?"

"From here, she went to Shreveport," Ackerman said. "She sent me a postcard and said she was working at a Cajun place. She needed more cash to get her to Dallas."

"Do you remember the name of that Cajun place?"

"Big Daddy's," Ackerman said, then a tense pause. "Chief?"

"Yeah?"

"I hope you find Honey."

"Thanks," John said. "If you think of anything else, anyone she might have mentioned being involved with after she left Alabama, please give me a call."

He gave Ackerman his number, then hung up.

"Anything?" Sam asked impatiently.

John shook his head. "Just like every other man who dated Honey, he worshiped the ground she walked on, and understood when she moved on."

Sam smiled, not surprised.

"When she left Alabama, she stopped in Shreveport and worked at a restaurant there. I'm going to find that number and give them a call."

Sam drained her coffee and set the cup on the steel table against the wall, then went to stare out the window while he searched the Internet for Big Daddy's.

A minute later, the manager came on the line, and John explained the reason for his call.

"I'm Big Daddy," the man said. "But Honey ain't worked here for over a year. She said she was moving to Dallas."

"Was she involved with anyone while she was there?"

Big Daddy sighed. "Yeah, she hooked up with one of my waiters for a while."

"Does he still work there?"

"Yeah, but he doesn't come in till the night shift."

"Would you give me his name and number so I can talk to him?"

"Sure thing. You really think someone hurt Honey?"

"It looks that way," John said, then scribbled down the other man's name and number. As soon as he disconnected the call with Big Daddy, he phoned Eric Cumberland. John let the phone ring and ring, and finally the man answered in a groggy voice.

"Who in the hell is this? It's eight o'clock in the damn morning."

John stiffened. "This is Police Chief John Wise calling from Georgia."

"Huh?"

He'd obviously woken the man. "Police Chief John Wise. I'm calling in reference to Honey Dawson."

A long pause, then he heard covers rustling. "Hang on a sec. Let me go in the other room."

John rapped his knuckles on the desk while he waited.

"What about Honey?" Cumberland asked. "Where is she?"

"I don't know, that's why I'm calling," John said, then explained the circumstances. "When did you last see or speak with her?"

Cumberland's voice became hushed as if someone else might be in the room and he wanted the conversation to remain private. "Oh, damn," he muttered. "Damn, I should have done something."

John's fingers tightened on the handset. This guy knew something. "What do you mean?"

Cumberland muttered a sound of frustration. "I haven't seen her since she moved to Dallas. But a couple of weeks ago, she called me and sounded upset."

"What did she say?"

"Not much," he said in a worried tone. "But I got the idea she was in trouble. She said she might need a place to stay."

"Did she come to Shreveport?"

"No," Cumberland said. "I'm dating another girl now, and she came in the room, and I told her I'd call Honey back. But I tried Honey later, and she didn't answer. I left her a message, but I never heard back."

John twisted his mouth in thought. "Do you know where she lived in Dallas?"

"Hang on another minute. Honey loved postcards and sent me one right after she moved. She wrote the address on the card."

Sam glanced at him impatiently while he waited, then Cumberland returned and gave him the address. "Chief?" Cumberland asked.

"Yes?"

"Please find her," Cumberland said. "I'd hate to think that anything bad happened to Honey."

John thanked him and hung up again, shaking his head at the man's response. Honey might love them and leave them, but so far, none of the men she'd left sounded as if they had a grudge.

The man after her had to be someone she'd met in Dallas.

Sam tapped her foot impatiently. "What did he say?"

"He gave me Honey's address in Dallas." He reached for his coat. "Let's go."

"Where to?" Sam asked.

"Dallas. If we find out what happened there, maybe we'll find the man after Honey."

Chapter Eleven

Sam had never been inside John's house. He lived in a small bungalow in town near the police station so he could be close to any call he received. Giant azaleas flanked the front with flowerbeds lining the walkway to the door and a huge magnolia in the front yard.

The home was unlike John's father's estate which sat on the edge of the town, property that backed up to the river and offered privacy as well as an aesthetic ambience that spoke of old money, power and prestige.

She suddenly felt odd, uneasy, without the baby in her arms and the buffer between them, as if being here in his home was invading his privacy.

And making her heart want to get closer to him.

The oak furnishings, knotty pine paneling and masculine colors seemed to suit him and differed from the ostentatious lifestyle and furnishings she'd imagined he'd grown up with. His mother had always stood by his father's side, a picture of support as he'd vaulted from police chief to mayor, launching him into a political future that included a senatorial run.

John's father had made no secret that he expected his son to follow in his footsteps. And so far, John had.

She reminded herself of the wide chasm between them and the differences in their goals. Butterville was the only home she'd known since Miss Mazie had taken her in, and she couldn't imagine living anywhere else.

Unlike Honey, who'd set her sights higher and had moved on.

Chocolate leather couches created an eye-catching, cozy place for conversation around the fireplace and plush pillows in blue and green served as accent pieces. She was slightly surprised but grateful not to find a moose or deer head on the wall like some of the hunters in the area sported and showed off.

John's footsteps pounded on the wood floor, and he clattered down the stairs carrying a duffel bag and his computer. "I called the airport and booked two flights. We'll stop by your house and you can pack."

She clutched her jacket around her and tried to banish the thought of the two of them sitting together on the couch in front of a raging fireplace, cozily snuggling up to each other as soft music played in the background. Then they'd kiss and finish what they'd started earlier, fall into bed and make love until dawn.

He frowned and gestured to the door, and she squashed those romantic thoughts. They had a plane to catch and a possible killer to find.

Criminal work was John's world, she thought as they hurried outside and into his car. A world she had been thrust into because of Honey, the little girl she'd left in her house and her missing son.

A world she wasn't sure she wanted to live in when the man after Honey was found.

Although by nature of her job, she would always deal

with the police. And John was the epitome of everything she admired....

But he was everything that she couldn't have.

Or wouldn't dare to hope for because the loss of loving someone would be too great, and she couldn't bear that kind of pain again.

JOHN REMAINED TENSE as he and Sam boarded the plane to Dallas. He had no idea what they might find and only hoped that Sam was up to the task.

That kiss with her earlier taunted him. Dammit, he wanted to kiss her again.

Thankfully, though, she had no idea the turmoil racking his mind. She had closed her eyes the minute the plane had departed and shut him out. He tried to do the same. He hadn't slept well here in two days and assured himself that the plane ride was his reprieve, so he adjusted his seat, leaned back and fell into a deep sleep.

The next thing he knew he jerked awake as the plane screeched to a stop on the runway. Through blurred eyes, he shifted and found Sam asleep on his shoulder, her pink lips parted, her fingers curled on his arm.

The picture was so seductive yet out of character for Sam that his heart swelled with protectiveness and an odd twinge he didn't recognize. A twinge that felt suddenly like—affection.

The flight attendant announced gates for connecting flights, and he gently shook Sam's arm to wake her. When she opened her eyes, she looked sleepy and trusting and so damn sexy that his chest clenched. For a brief second, he allowed himself to imagine that this was a vacation, an intimate interlude they'd planned together, not an investigation into the stalking and possible death of her best friend.

"John?"

"We're in Dallas," he said. "The plane just landed."

Silently, like the strong person she'd always been, she gathered her composure, then they retrieved their bags from the overhead carrier and followed the train of passengers out. A half hour later, they'd commandeered a rental car and driven straight to the address Honey's friend had given them for her last residence in Dallas. It was a small apartment building on the edge of the city that looked as if it had seen better days.

Sunshine glinted through the trees as he and Sam climbed out, the afternoon heat warmer in Dallas than the mountains of Georgia, the land flatter, the absence of storms a welcome reprieve.

Sam followed behind him quietly, the tension building as they approached the apartment door. He knocked, but as they'd expected, no one answered, so after a few minutes, they went in search of the super of the complex.

An older white-haired man grunted as he answered the door. "What?"

John flashed his ID. "We're looking into the disappearance of one of your tenants. A lady named Honey Dawson."

The chubby man scratched his belly. "But you're not with the Dallas Police."

"No," John said. "But a girl who lives in your complex is missing, perhaps dead. Now all we want is for you to answer some questions."

The man's unibrow pushed upward. "All right. Hell, I hate to think anything happened to Honey. She was a damn sweet girl."

So sweet that someone wanted her dead.

John wanted to roll his eyes; like every other male he'd encountered so far, the super was completely enamored with Honey.

"Could you let us into her apartment?" he asked. "There might be something in there that could help us locate her."

The man frowned.

"Please, sir." Sam touched his elbow. "Honey was my best friend and I'm worried about her."

The super shrugged, reached for the set of keys clipped to his belt and gestured for them to follow. John surveyed the weathered building and overgrown grounds. The inside of the apartment needed fresh paint and the furnishings were minimal. An old dog-eared TV sat on a rickety stand, a brown plaid sofa and recliner provided seating and the kitchen cabinets were a cheap wood.

"Lock the door when you leave," the man said, then lumbered away.

Sam walked over to the table next to the sofa, picked up a picture frame and flipped it around to show him. "Look, John, here's a photograph of Honey holding the babies in the hospital. This proves that Emmie is hers."

"It's not proof," John said. "But it does look that way."

He started searching the desk drawers. There was no computer, but he found an unpaid phone bill and electric bill inside the top drawer. Stacks of paid bills filled a file, then he found a series of bank statements. He frowned. There were several overdrawn statements from prior months, but a recent statement revealed a rather large deposit. Ten grand.

A lot for a waitress to accumulate in a short time.

"Did you find something?" Sam asked over his shoulder.

He gestured at the statement. "It looks as if Honey was struggling financially, but lately she came into some money."

Sam clamped her lower lip with her teeth as if she understood the implications. Honey might have gotten into something illegal.

Sam went into the bedroom, and he continued to search through the desk, looking for notes, a journal, anything to indicate who she might have been involved with. Sam returned a few minutes later.

"Did you find anything?" he asked.

A troubled look crossed her face. "You said Honey had some overdrawn slips and a ten thousand dollar deposit. It's odd but there are some really nice clothes in her closet."

"Why is that odd?"

"They don't look like something Honey would choose for herself. She liked glitz and glamour but where did she get that money in the bank and these clothes?"

John frowned, his mind working. She wasn't going to like his train of thought. "Maybe she had a sugar daddy."

"No," Sam said instantly, although he sensed that deep down she had probably contemplated the possibility herself.

A knock sounded on the opened door, and John and Sam looked up to see a short, voluptuous Hispanic girl standing in the doorway.

"What are you two doing in Honey's apartment?"

John flashed his badge. "We're looking for information about Honey Dawson. Did you know her?"

"Yes." Her brown eyes widened in concern. "Why? What happened to her?"

"That's what we're trying to find out," John said. "What's your name, miss?"

The woman shifted and leaned against the door. "Roberta Frontera."

Sam cleared her throat and moved toward the woman, gesturing for her to come in. "Honey and I grew up together," she said. "We've been best friends since we were children. A couple of days ago she came to my house with Emmie, but I wasn't home at the time. When I arrived, Honey was gone, but I found blood on the floor and her little girl in my closet. It looked as if there had been a struggle."

"Oh my." Roberta clutched the wall and muttered a few words in Spanish. "I was afraid something bad had happened."

"Why would you think that?" Sam asked.

She sighed and tucked a strand of her wavy brown hair behind one ear. "Because she was here one night, then the next I saw her rushing from her apartment in the middle of the night like the devil was on her heels."

"Do you know of anyone who would want to hurt her?" John asked.

Roberta fidgeted. "There was this Peeping Tom a while back who broke into her apartment and stole her underwear. She called the police and filed charges. I think they even went to court."

HONEY HAD A PEEPING TOM? A stalker?

Sam glanced at John. "Do you know this guy's name or where he is now?"

Roberta shook her head no. "She didn't say his

name. But he was in jail for a while. I don't know if he got out or not."

"Thanks," John said. "That's very helpful and will give us a place to look."

"Was there anything else strange going on with Honey?" Sam asked.

Roberta twisted her mouth in thought. "Well, for a while Honey was struggling to make ends meet. But the last month or two she started wearing nicer clothes and jewelry. But she never said how she got the money."

Sam contemplated the large deposit in Honey's account and wondered where it had come from. "Was she dating anyone?"

Roberta flipped her hair over her shoulder. "This guy Jimmy hung around a lot. I think she met him at court. He was a bailiff or something like that."

"Do you know his last name?" John asked.

"I'm afraid not."

Sam gave her an imploring look. "You knew Honey had twins?"

Roberta nodded. "*Sí*. She was so proud of those babies. I hope they're all right. Honey loved them so much."

"Was this man Jimmy the father of the twins?" John asked.

Roberta shrugged. "I have no idea. She never told me. But Jimmy was completely taken with Honey. He helped her through the pregnancy. I think he would have married her if she'd said yes."

"We have to find him," Sam said to John.

John nodded and thanked Roberta. "Let's go pay the police department a visit and find out about this stalker first."

Roberta left, and they locked up, then rushed to the

rental car. John consulted his PDA for an address for the police department and steered them into town. Sam had never been to Dallas, but she was too preoccupied with thoughts of Honey to enjoy the scenery. Still the high-rise office buildings, storefronts and throngs of people seemed daunting compared to the small town of Butterville.

John parked at the station on Lamar Street, the afternoon sun beating down on them as they entered the station. He showed his ID to the receptionist when they entered and explained the reason for their visit. Five minutes later, they were led through security past a bullpen housing various desks, computers and officers to a private office.

A medium height, craggy-looking man with short wavy brown hair stood, tugging at his pants. "I'm Detective Arnold."

"Police Chief John Wise and Samantha Corley." Once again John explained the situation and what they'd learned so far. "Can you tell us about the man who was stalking Honey?"

The detective pulled his hand down his chin, then opened his filing cabinet, rooted around and removed a file with a labored sigh. He returned to his desk, sat down and spread it open.

"The stalker's name was Neil Kinney."

"Tell us more," John said. "When did this stalking occur?"

"Let's see. Honey said she moved to town late May, early June. He started stalking her, then broke into her apartment and stole her underwear."

"And she filed a report?"

"Yes. We placed a restraining order on him at first, but after the break-in, we pressed charges. Honey testified for the grand jury in August."

"And Kinney went to jail?"

"Yes," Detective Arnold said, then pinched his lips together in a frown.

"What is it?" Sam asked.

He released a frustrated breath. "Unfortunately the man was released a month ago. I notified Honey so she would be aware and told her to let me know if he bothered her again."

"And did she?" John asked.

He shook his head. "But if Honey is missing or hurt, I would definitely look at him as a suspect. He was pretty ticked off when she testified against him and threatened to make her pay when he got out."

Chapter Twelve

John contemplated the fact that Honey had a stalker, and that Kinney was out of prison now. Detective Arnold was right. Kinney could have gone after her.

Based on the profile of a typical stalker, he was obsessed with Honey, and in his twisted mind probably imagined that she and he had a relationship. Knowing she'd been with other men, that she'd been carrying another man's babies, might have driven him over the edge.

But why hurt the babies?

"Do you know where Neil Kinney is now?" John asked. "Is there an address or a family member's house where he would go?"

The detective consulted the file. "No current one, and no relatives listed. But his parole officer should know. If he's left the state, he's violated parole. And if he even got near Honey, he'll go back to jail."

"Thank you." John stood. "By the way, which Judge oversaw the case?"

Again, the detective glanced at the files. "Judge Teddy Wexler. You can find him at the courthouse."

John gave him his card, and Sam thanked him,

then they left the precinct and headed to the courthouse. Again they went through security, and John met with a court clerk and explained the reason for their visit.

"I'm afraid Judge Wexler is in court at the moment," the clerk said. "But if you want to wait, I'll let him know you're here."

"Of course," John said. "Does he have a bailiff named Jimmy?"

The clerk smiled. "Oh, yes, that would be Jimmy Bartow. He's a great guy, and a hard worker."

"I need to speak with him, as well."

"All right. I'll have one of the other clerks show you to the office beside the judge's chambers where you can wait."

They followed the clerk through the mammoth building to the office and were seated in plush chairs in the corner near a receptionist's desk where they were left stewing for half an hour. Finally the judge agreed to see them. Sam introduced them as they entered his chambers.

"I take it you know who I am." Judge Wexler extended his hand to shake Sam's, then John's.

The judge's confident swagger boasted of arrogance. The dark mahogany paneling gave his chambers a richness that spoke of money, and a huge desk dominated the room with a stocked liquor cabinet and dozens of photographs of the judge's commendations lined the walls. A trophy case held various awards and pictures of a younger man, Teddy Jr., who resembled the judge and his high school football championship awards.

Another photograph of an attractive woman sat on the judge's desk, a stylish blonde decked out in jewels and designer wear who looked fragile but well kept. "My wife, Portia," Judge Wexler said with a proud grin. "She's lovely, isn't she? She was Miss Texas when we met."

"She is lovely," Sam agreed, and John nodded.

"So, what can I do for you, Chief Wise? You're not exactly in your own territory."

John studied the man's cool facade. "Judge, do you remember a woman named Honey Dawson?"

Judge Wexler cocked his head sideways. "Dawson?"

"Yes," John said. "Blond, good-looking."

Wexler made a clicking sound with his teeth. "Of course. She was in my court. Testified against a man named Kinney for breaking into her apartment. He was stalking her, stole her underwear and took a plea bargain on a burglary charge."

"That's right," John said.

"Why are you asking about Miss Dawson?" Judge Wexler asked.

John and Sam traded looks, then John spoke. "She's missing, Judge. Two days ago, she came to Georgia, and hasn't been seen or heard from since."

Sam explained her relationship with Honey and the blood on the floor. "She left her little girl at my house."

The corner of the judge's mouth thinned as he turned to stare at Sam. "She left a baby at your house."

"Yes," Sam said. "But we saw a photograph of twins in her apartment, so now we're wondering what happened to the little boy."

The judge maintained a steady gaze. "You think Kinney hurt Honey and the baby boy?"

Sam made a noncommittal sound. "I don't know," Sam said.

"That's why we're here," John said. "We're trying to

track down Honey's movements the last few months and hope to get a lead on someone who wanted to hurt her."

"The only person I can think of is Kinney," Judge Wexler said. "Have you talked to the Dallas police?"

"Yes, they're looking for him now," John said.

The judge stood. "Then I don't know how I can help you."

John hesitated. Something about the judge seemed off. He was too nice, charming, quick to dismiss them. "Did you ever see Honey after the trial?"

Wexler squared his shoulders as if to intimidate John. He must be a formidable man to cross, a man who obviously liked his power and position.

"Of course not." Wexler glanced at his wife's picture. "I'm a married man, Chief Wise. A wealthy man with power in this town. I would never do anything to jeopardize my reputation."

John didn't believe him. "We'd like to see your bailiff Jimmy Bartow now."

The judge shuffled papers on his desk. "He's gone for the day."

"Then we'll visit him at home. We heard he and Honey were friends. Maybe he can tell us who followed her to town and assaulted her."

Judge Wexler's composed face slipped again, slight, but John homed in on it.

"Can you give me his address?" John asked.

"Ask my receptionist," the judge said. "Although take whatever he says with a grain of salt. Jimmy's a decent bailiff, but he's had his fair share of problems with women."

"What do you mean?" John asked.

Judge Wexler shrugged. "I mean, he's intense and he has a temper."

SAM FOLDED HER ARMS as they left Judge Wexler's office. "What do you think?"

John sighed, placed a hand to the back of her waist and waited until they were in the hallway before he spoke. "I think he's the first man we've spoken with who hasn't admitted he was enamored with Honey." His eyes darkened. "And that makes him look suspicious."

Sam's mouth quirked into a smile. "Honey did have that effect on men."

"Not everyone," he said, and her brows pinched together in question.

"You can't tell me that you didn't think she was beautiful," Sam said.

He shrugged. "Physically yes, but there are other beautiful women in the world, Sam. Some who appeal to me more."

Her heart fluttered in her chest as his gaze met hers. The kiss they'd shared taunted her.

A look akin to hunger flared in his eyes as if he too remembered the titillating moment, and heat climbed her face. A small smile curved his mouth, and he reached up to tweak her hair, but a man in a bailiff uniform, black pants, black jacket, black shirt, black tie, badge on his jacket pocket and ID card pinned to his lapel appeared and cleared his throat.

"Are you that cop from Georgia?"

John jerked his head to the side. "Yes. And you are?"

The uniformed man jammed his hands in his pockets. "Jimmy Bartow. I heard you were asking questions about Honey."

"Yes," John said. "And we thought you'd left for the day. Is there someplace we can go to talk?"

The bailiff nodded and led them through a corridor and

down a hall into a small holding room, which Sam knew from experience was reserved for questioning potential jurors. As soon as the door closed, Jimmy began to pace.

Judge Wexler's comment about Jimmy echoed in Sam's head. He said Jimmy was intense and had a temper. He also said Jimmy was gone for the day. Had the judge lied to keep them from questioning Jimmy?

Had Jimmy followed Honey and hurt her? And if so, why?

A power and calmness radiated from John as he claimed a seat in one of the hardback chairs, crossed his arms and waited. His ironclad control was intimidating.

"All right, Jimmy," John said. "Tell us about your relationship with Honey."

Jimmy scrubbed his hand through his hair, spiking the ends. "Did something happen to Honey?"

"We don't know. That's why we're here," Sam said softly. "I'm Honey's friend and we're looking for her."

"But you came all the way from Georgia. So you know something?" Jimmy leaned against the chair and jiggled his leg. "I've been so worried about her. She just up and ran off and didn't tell me. I don't know why Honey would do that, leave without telling me."

"So you and Honey were close?" John asked.

Jimmy nodded. "I cared about Honey. We were good friends."

"But you wanted more, didn't you?" John asked. "You were in love with Honey?"

Jimmy twitched, then picked at an imaginary piece of lint on his pants leg. "Everyone loved Honey."

John stood, looking imposing at six foot three as he stared down at Jimmy. "Maybe. But someone tried to kill her, and they may have succeeded." He punctuated his comment with an accusing stare. "So did Honey turn down your advances, Jimmy? Did she tell you she didn't want you, so you got pissed off and she left town to get away from you?"

Jimmy's eyes widened with shock. "What? Who told you such a thing?"

"We know you were at Honey's place. And we heard you have a temper," John said.

"Me?" Jimmy seemed genuinely stunned that he was a suspect. "No, you've got it all wrong. Honey and I were friends. Friends, I tell you." He slumped into a chair and jammed his hands in his pockets again. "I admit that I was in love with her, and wanted her to see me that way, but I understood she couldn't." He turned an imploring look toward Sam. "I decided that I'd take whatever Honey had to give me. Anything, just to be near her."

The poor guy, Sam thought. Honey had no idea how she affected men. That she broke their hearts when she moved from one to the other.

"What happened, Jimmy?" Sam asked.

The bailiff sighed and blew into his hands. "We met when she testified against the grand jury last year. But she was seeing someone else, some guy named Reed Tanner. Only he moved to California, and Honey was upset so we spent one night together." His faraway smile told Sam it was a fond memory.

"But Honey wanted more," Jimmy continued. "She wanted that cheerleading spot and money and…all the things I couldn't give her."

"Did you know that Honey's stalker was out of prison?" John asked. "Did she say anything about hearing from him or seeing him?"

He shook his head. "No, I didn't know that creep

was out of jail. But he sure freaked Honey out. He was a psycho."

John and Sam exchanged looks, and Sam's stomach clenched.

"Is there anyone else you can think of who would hurt Honey?" John asked. "Did she have any other enemies?"

Jimmy fidgeted with his ID again, hesitating. "Yeah. This girl on the cheerleading spot. Honey said she was jealous as hell of her, and that they were fighting for the same spot."

Sam closed her eyes, imagining the situation. The men loved Honey, the women hated her.

"What was her name?" John asked.

Jimmy tapped his mouth, thinking. "Seems like it was Tiffany something. Oh, Tiffany Maylor. Her daddy had a boatload of money. He's in jewelry or something like that."

John scribbled her name on his notepad. "How about the judge?" he asked. "Did he and Honey ever have a personal relationship?"

Jimmy jiggled his leg again. "Yeah. After we were together that night, they had an affair. But Judge Wexler was an ass to Honey, and she broke it off. I overhead the judge and his son arguing about Honey one day after he found out she was pregnant."

"So the judge's son knew about the twins?" Sam asked.

Jimmy bobbed his head up and down. "Yeah, and he didn't like it. Said they weren't the judge's and that the judge should get rid of Honey."

"The judge wanted her to keep quiet about the babies and the affair?" John asked.

"Yeah." Jimmy shrugged. "Honey was afraid he

would try to take the twins away from her. He owns half the town here and has enough power to do it."

"Is he the father of the twins?" John asked.

"I don't know for sure," Jimmy said. "Could have been that Tanner guy's, I guess, that is, if they'd hooked back up. But Wexler thought the twins were his."

"Judge Wexler lied to us," Sam said.

John muttered a low curse. "Yes, and we're going to talk to him again."

"Do you think the judge would hurt Honey to get to the babies?" Sam asked.

"Maybe," Jimmy said in a pained voice. "He puts on a charming face, but anybody who's seen him in court knows he's ruthless."

"So, now we have four suspects," John said. "Honey's stalker, Neil Kinney. Honey's rival for the cheerleading spot. Judge Wexler. And Wexler's son, Teddy Jr."

"This is unbelievable," Sam whispered. "And we need to talk to that guy Reed Tanner."

"We've certainly got our work cut out." John turned to Sam. "First, let's talk to the judge again. The fact that he lied to our faces suggests he's hiding something. And if that gorgeous wife of his found out about the judge's extracurricular affairs, we can add her to the suspect list."

Sam gritted her teeth. Honey had gathered a lot of enemies since she'd left Butterville. Which one of them wanted her dead?

Chapter Thirteen

John grimaced. Honey Dawson had gotten herself in one fine mess. If they found her alive, he was tempted to shake the little vixen for tossing Sam into the middle of her problems.

"Do you know where we can find Reed Tanner?" he asked.

A muscle twitched in Jimmy's jaw. "No. But he still owns a ranch around Springton, I think. Where are the twins now?"

John glanced at Sam, silently warning her not to say too much. At this point, he didn't know whom they could trust. "The baby girl is safe," John said. "We don't know about the little boy. Do you know where he is?"

Jimmy began to pace again. "No. Gosh, I don't understand why Honey didn't come to me. She knew I'd do anything for her. I would have taken care of her and the twins." He halted and ground his toe into the carpet. "But Judge Wexler, he treated her like a tramp. He tried to bribe her to get rid of the babies. And God knows, he has enough money in his pockets to do it. Everyone around these parts knows about the Wexler

Ranch. He's got two outdoor pools and an indoor one, tennis courts and a damn football field in back that he built for his precious son Teddy Jr. so he could practice when he was in high school."

"Jimmy, please let us know if you hear from Honey, or if you learn something that could help us," Sam said.

"Of course." Worry strained his features. "Let me know when you find her. I can't stand to think that anything bad happened to her or those babies."

John left him his card, and the two of them headed back toward the judge's chambers.

"I don't understand why Judge Wexler lied," Sam said. "Didn't he realize that Jimmy would tell us about the affair?"

"Jimmy works for the judge," John said. "Maybe Wexler thought he would be too afraid to talk."

"Jimmy obviously cares enough about Honey that fear didn't stop him."

"Yeah, Jimmy was a wealth of information," John said with a brisk shake of his head.

They arrived back at the receptionist, and John cleared his throat. "We need to see Judge Wexler again."

The receptionist gestured toward the door. "You just missed him. He left to go home."

John frowned. "Then we need his address."

She hesitated, but John leaned against the desk, his tone commanding. "This is an official police investigation, miss. I'm sure the judge would want you to cooperate."

Her brow pinched together, then she scribbled Wexler's address on a sticky note. He took it then led Sam out of the building. Sam lapsed into silence on the way to the Wexler Ranch, while John considered the number of suspects they were racking up. Hopefully, Detective Arnold would locate Neil Kinney. Meanwhile, he wanted to talk to all the other players in Honey's little drama.

The Wexler Ranch was just as he'd expected—impressive. The white house looked stately, like a miniature White House, the fence and corrals made of white wood instead of the normal steel pipe coral fencing and electric/barbed wire used for the pastures.

The arrogant man was flaunting his wealth.

That arrogance suggested he would probably do anything to keep his secrets and preserve his reputation. That ten thousand dollar deposit in Honey's account would have been a drop in the bucket for him—maybe he'd tried to bribe Honey not to tell his wife about the affair or the twins.

And if Honey had stepped in his way and decided to do that...

"HE'D BETTER TELL US the truth this time." Sam reached for the car door handle. The sun was beginning to slip and cast shadows across the rolling green pastures as they parked in the circular drive and walked up to the door.

"I doubt he'll admit to hurting Honey," John said. "But maybe he'll slip and implicate himself. I want to talk to his wife and son, too."

Sam's worried gaze swung to his. "You're right. If one of them knew about the affair and babies, they might have tried to shut Honey up."

John rang the doorbell and they waited in tense silence until the door opened. A maid wearing a nametag that read Louisa greeted them. "How can I help you?"

John flashed his ID. "We need to speak to Judge Wexler."

"He just arrived home. Can I tell him who's calling?"

"He knows who I am," John said.

Sam studied the foyer. The inside was gilded with expensive crown moldings, ornate rugs, paintings and furnishings. The richness of his mansion astounded her.

A second later, the judge appeared, this time without his judge's robe, although still in a pricey designer suit. He cradled a glass of bourbon in his hand and steered them toward his study. Rich paneling surrounded the room with a state-of-the-art computer system and desk dominating the area. Built-in cherry bookcases held an assortment of law journals and leather-bound books.

"You knew we'd be back," John said.

The judge shrugged, then gestured toward the built-in bar. "Would you like a drink?"

"No," John said. "We want answers."

"Why did you lie?" Sam asked.

"You came to my chambers and asked private questions. I have a reputation to protect."

"But you knew we'd find out the truth," John said. "That you and Honey had an affair."

The judge sighed wearily and sank into his leather chair. "That was a long time ago. It's been over forever and was a mistake."

"Does your wife know?" John asked.

The judge sipped his bourbon. "Yes. But that stupid bailiff is the one you should look at. He was obsessed with Honey and hated any man that even looked at her."

"That's not the way Jimmy tells it," John said. "Jimmy said that he heard you and your son arguing about Honey's pregnancy. That you tried to bribe her to get rid of the babies."

Anger flashed in Wexler's eyes, and he drummed his

fingers on the desk. "That's not true. I thought the twins were mine and wanted to take care of them, to raise them the way a Wexler should be raised. Then Honey just up and disappeared." The ice clinked in his highball glass as he drained the rest of the bourbon. "I even hired a private investigator to find her, but so far, he hasn't reported anything."

"So you admit that you had an affair, that you think the twins are yours and you want them?" John asked.

Judge Wexler set his glass down with a clink. "Yes."

"But Honey didn't want you, did she?" Sam said. "She turned you down and you got angry and were going to take the babies from her."

The judge fixed his gaze on Sam, then gestured around the room. "Look at this place. If I want something, I have enough money and power in this town to get it. I certainly wouldn't need to resort to violence."

Rage heated Sam's blood. "Honey figured that out and told you to get lost, didn't she? She didn't want an arrogant man like you around her children."

A coldness settled in the judge's steely blue eyes. "Those babies are mine, and as soon as my people find them, they will be raised as Wexlers, not by a whore like Honey."

"And your wife and son are on board with that?" John asked.

The judge cut his gaze toward John. "I'm Teddy Wexler. My wife and son will do whatever I tell them."

JOHN HAD SEEN A LOT of arrogant men in his time, but Teddy Wexler was the biggest narcissist he'd met to date. He might put on a charming face to the public, but the judge was ruthless.

No wonder Honey had run. He could squash her like a bug.

And he'd probably treated her like one, too. Romanced her, wined and dined her, gave her gifts, and when she'd gotten pregnant, he'd threatened her, bribed her, then...

Then what?

He wouldn't have muddied his hands by going after her personally. No, the man was too cunning and smart. He had so much money he'd hire someone to take care of his dirty business. With his connections as a judge, he would also have access to men who would do anything for money—or a favor in the legal department.

"Where is your wife now?" he asked. "We'd like to talk to her."

"That's not possible at the moment. She's at a private day spa getting the works today. It's my treat for our anniversary."

"Then tomorrow." John stood. "How about your son?"

"You don't need to speak to him," Wexler said.

John arched a brow. "I'll decide that. Where does he live?"

"In a condo downtown," the judge answered. "But Teddy didn't do anything to Honey Dawson. He's a good boy."

A sardonic smile touched John's face. "Then there's no reason you'd mind me talking to him."

Wexler rose, then braced his hands on his desk. "Why don't you go back to your little town and let us take care of things here, Chief."

John's jaw tightened. "I'll go home when I have the answers I came for."

He took Sam's elbow and led her to the door. "We'll be back tomorrow to speak to your wife. And all your money and power won't stop me from finding the truth, Wexler."

Wexler slammed the door behind them and they went to the car.

"I don't like him," Sam said as she settled in the seat. "And I don't believe him. Why would a powerful man like him want his affair exposed? It seems he wouldn't have wanted his wife to know that he'd slept with Honey, especially that she'd given birth to his children."

John started the engine and drove toward downtown Dallas. The last strains of the sun had faded, night was approaching, the long day wearing on them both. "I have to admit that is odd. Maybe Honey told his wife and that pissed him off, and he came after her. He could be lying about wanting to raise the babies as his."

They lapsed into another tense silence until they arrived at the multimillion dollar condominium complex, a high-rise modern structure that towered over neighboring buildings, but one that, according to the signs, boasted indoor and outdoor swimming pools, tennis courts, workout facilities, spas, restaurants and bars, as well as an underground exclusive shopping center.

A virtual minicity within itself.

John parked in the parking deck, then they entered the building, and stopped at the security desk. Modern overhead lighting, sleek marble floors and contemporary paintings added ambience. The setup appeared to cater to a younger posh sect, leaving the rugged ranch life behind.

John explained to the tall bald attendant at the desk that he needed to see Teddy Wexler Jr.

"You must be here for his party. Let me buzz him on his intercom." The attendant flipped a switch and announced them. "Mr. Wexler, you have two more guests."

Seconds later, Teddy Jr.'s Texas drawl echoed back. "All right, send them up."

"Unit 2304." The attendant gestured toward the bank of elevators to the right. John punched the up button. Steel doors slid open, and he and Sam climbed inside.

The elevator stopped twice to let on others, then finally they arrived and walked down a plush carpeted hallway to the unit on the end. Loud music rocked the walls, the sound of voices and laughter filling the hallway.

John knocked on a steel door, and it slid open. Teddy Wexler, a younger version of his father, stood in the entryway dressed in a fancy black button-up shirt and designer jeans with silver-studded cowboy boots, a bourbon in his hand. Behind him, the room was packed with guests drinking, laughing and dancing.

Teddy Jr.'s drunken smile faded slightly at the sight of John's badge, then his gaze roved over Sam and a leer lit his eyes.

John sized him up immediately. Cocky, lazy, spoiled, rich, and judging from the way his gaze roved over Sam and lingered on her breasts, a damn womanizer. He was also sporting a bruised nose and a scrape on his right hand.

The son of a bitch could take his eyes off Sam. She wasn't up for grabs.

The thought momentarily stunned him. He had no claims on Sam, so why should it bother him if another man looked at her?

Teddy extended his hand to Sam and introduced himself. "Well, hello there, sugar. Aren't you a sight for sore eyes?"

Sam stiffened and pulled her hand away. "The name is Samantha Corley."

"Samantha," he said in a low murmur. "Nice to meet you."

John cleared his throat. "I'm Chief of Police John Wise, from Georgia."

Teddy's mouth thinned as he shook his hand. "What's a Georgia cop doing all the way here in Texas crashing my party?"

"We're here about Honey Dawson," Sam cut in, obviously seeing Teddy Jr. for the leech he was.

Teddy swung his gaze to her again, a look of displeasure clearly shadowing his face. So he wasn't as adept at acting as his father. Behind him, John noticed a beautiful brunette watching. She started toward them, but Teddy Jr. stepped into the hallway and pushed the door shut to keep out prying eyes as he confronted them. "As you can see, I'm busy."

"We just want you to answer a couple of questions," John said smoothly. "If you have nothing to hide, then that shouldn't be a problem."

Teddy sipped his drink. "Why would you think I know anything about that woman?"

"Cut the crap," John said. "We've talked to your father. We know he and Honey had an affair and that the twins she gave birth to might have been his. He admitted that he hired a private investigator to find her."

Teddy's brown brow shot up. "And has he found her?"

"That's why we're here," John said. "We think someone followed her all the way to Georgia to Miss Corley's house, and tried to kill her."

Teddy leaned against the wall. "Well, it's no wonder. Honey was a two-bit tramp who'd spread her legs for any guy in pants. I'm sure she ticked off a lot of people."

"How about you?" John asked. "Did she tick you off by sleeping with your father?"

"I don't care who the hell my old man bangs," Teddy said. "We both like women."

"And your father liked Honey," John said. "How did your father feel about her pregnancy?"

Teddy shrugged. "Dad tried to help the bitch because he felt sorry for her. He even gave her some money for those brats, but she wanted more. She would have milked him for everything he had if he let her."

"So you're admitting you had a motive to hurt her?" John said.

Teddy clamped his mouth shut, then said, "No, I'm just telling you the facts."

"This is what I think happened." John poked Teddy's chest with his finger. "Your father wanted to keep Honey quiet about the babies. And you didn't want to share Daddy's money with anyone, especially Honey and her twins, so one or both of you conspired to get rid of her."

"For your information, the money Dad gave Honey was nothing to us," Teddy said snidely. "And I wouldn't fool with hurting that bitch. She's not worth the trouble."

John folded his arms. Teddy could be lying. "How did you get those bruises, Teddy?"

Teddy fidgeted and rubbed at his nose. "A fight."

"You mean a barroom brawl?"

He shook his head. "Hell, no. The son of a bitch you should be talking to, Reed Tanner. That hothead was here earlier and crashed my party."

"And you two got into a fight?"

He nodded. "Tanner was jealous of me back in high school because I landed the quarterback position over him, and tonight he attacked me."

"He attacked you for something that happened years ago?" John asked. "I'm not buying that."

Teddy jammed his free hand in his pocket. "Well, believe it. Tanner's hated me ever since. He and Honey had a fling before she moved on to screw my old man. Maybe those babies are his, and he killed her because she tried to milk him for money, too. Hell, she might have been blackmailing a half dozen other guys for all I know."

John studied him for a long moment. He didn't totally believe Teddy was innocent, but Jimmy Bartow had also mentioned Reed Tanner, so he had to check him out, too.

John glanced down at Teddy's shoes. They were just about the same size as the boot prints outside Sam's house, but these were expensive cowboy boots, and the prints at Sam's had looked like work boots. Would Wexler even own a pair of work boots?

He needed a warrant to search Teddy's and take his DNA and prints. "Where were you three nights ago?"

Teddy's face grew pinched. "Right here in Dallas. My mom and I had dinner that night. You can ask her yourself."

"I'll do that," John said. "And if you had anything to do with Honey's disappearance or if you tried to hurt her babies, I will find out, Teddy. And this time your daddy's money won't save your butt or keep you out of jail. Nothing will."

Chapter Fourteen

Sam had just reached the car when the sound of a gun firing rent the air. She screamed as the bullet zinged by her head.

"Get down!" John shouted.

Her pulse jumped as she ducked beside the car, her chest heaving as she searched the shadows of the parking deck. Bright headlights from a car to the right nearly blinded her, and another shot rang out, hitting the windshield of a sedan to their left.

John crouched beside her, removed his gun from the holster, then inched his head up to see over the car. "Dammit, I can't see him."

Another shot hit the roof of their car, and she grabbed John's arm. "Get down, he's going to kill you!"

John squeezed her hand, but gently pried it loose. "Sam, stay here and stay low, I'm going after him."

"No," she whispered. "It's too dangerous."

He ignored her, then wove between the parked cars, crouching as he ran. Another bullet zoomed by, and hit the concrete, and she held her breath, praying it missed. John fired back this time, and she saw a shadow move. Footsteps pounded the pavement, then the sound of a car engine firing up echoed off the concrete walls of the deck.

Tires screeched, more headlights flooded the darkness, then the car raced by, firing once more at her before it shot out into the street.

Sam clutched the door handle, trembling as John ran back toward her, then clicked the automatic keypad to unlock the doors. "Get in, Sam!"

She threw open the door and jumped inside, reaching for her seat belt as John started the car, hit the gas and spun them forward. Their tires squealed as he careened from the parking deck, and he raced onto the street. But a red light caught them, hemming them in downtown traffic, and up ahead the shooter disappeared into the night.

"Damn," John muttered, then slapped the steering wheel with his hand. "I couldn't get a license plate."

"Do you think that was Teddy Jr. firing at us?" Sam asked.

A muscle ticked in his jaw. "I don't know. If it was, he got downstairs awfully fast."

"Maybe that guy Reed Tanner was still hanging around," Sam suggested.

"It's possible." John pulled at his chin. "Although for a moment when I was chasing the shooter, I thought it might have been a woman."

"A woman?" Sam pursed her lips. "Maybe Judge Wexler's wife?"

John shrugged. "I didn't get a good look. And we still haven't talked to that cheerleader Tiffany Maylor."

"Then let's go talk to her," Sam said.

"I'll see if Detective Arnold can get me a search warrant for Wexler's place, and for his prints. If we find a gun that matches those bullet casings we can bring him in for questioning and pressure him to talk."

He circled back around the block, drove back into the deck, then pulled on gloves and grabbed a flashlight from the trunk. "Let me find the bullet casings so I can have them analyzed. If we can trace the gun, maybe we'll find out who's doing this."

Sam stared out the window as he searched. If Teddy Wexler owned half of the town and was as powerful as everyone implied, would they be able to find a judge who would sign a search warrant for his son's condo?

JOHN PHONED DETECTIVE ARNOLD and explained about the shooting.

Detective Arnold made a low sound in his throat. "Bring the bullets by and I'll have our crime lab process them."

"Good. Have you located Neil Kinney yet?" John asked.

"We're working on it."

John explained about his conversation with Judge Wexler and his son. "I need a warrant for Teddy Jr.'s condo and car," John said.

Detective Arnold released a low whistle. "Judge Wexler is well known and respected around here. It won't be easy to find another judge who'll cross him, especially without more to go on than you have."

John gritted his teeth. One thing he hated about politics—even in a town this big, money bred power and people could be bought.

"Well, see what you can do anyway," he said. "I need another favor."

A long sigh. "What?"

"Find an address on a woman named Tiffany Maylor. She and Honey were competing for the same cheerleader spot."

"You think a girl would try to kill someone over cheerleading tryouts?"

John shrugged. The high school girls had certainly gotten into some nasty cat fights during competition. One his junior year had even ended up in the hospital. "I'm just checking out all leads."

"Hang on," Detective Arnold said.

John patted the steering wheel while he waited, and glanced at Sam. She looked exhausted and worried, and he considered taking her to a hotel room while he went to question Tiffany. But after that close call earlier, he couldn't leave her alone.

Detective Arnold came back on the line and gave him an address for an apartment near the football stadium, and John thanked him, then steered the rental car toward the apartment. Tiffany's dwellings were nothing like Teddy's—she lived in an older white house that had been divided into apartments. He parked on the side street, then he and Sam climbed out and walked up the sidewalk to the front. He checked the numbers and found Tiffany's, then knocked. Country music floated from the house, and a light switched on in the foyer, then a young redhead wearing a tank top and exercise shorts opened the door.

"Tiffany Maylor?" John asked.

The petite redhead removed the earphone from her iPod. "No, I'm Cara, Tiffany's roommate." She gestured toward a large framed photo of a dark brunette wearing a cheerleading outfit on the wall. "That's Tiff."

"Where is she?" John asked.

Cara twisted her mouth sideways. "Who wants to know?"

John flashed his ID. "We need to question her about a woman who's missing. Did you know Honey Dawson?"

Cara bit her lip. "Good grief, you're the second person who's been asking about that girl."

"Who else asked?" John asked.

"Some guy named Reed Tanner and a female P.I."

"You didn't answer my question," John said. "Did you know her?"

"She tried out for the cheerleading squad like Tiffany. I heard Tiff talk about her, but I never met her."

"So you weren't at tryouts?" Sam asked.

Cara laughed. "No way, I'm in college studying pre-med."

"Tiffany didn't like Honey, did she?" John asked.

Cara waved a hand dismissively. "They were competing for the same spot. Claws come out, but that doesn't mean Tiffany would hurt Honey. She got the spot fair and square when Honey was cut."

"Where is Tiffany now?" John asked again.

Cara sighed. "She had practice earlier, then showered and went to a party."

"Where is the party?" John asked.

"Teddy Wexler's condo."

"She knows Teddy?" Sam asked, her gaze swinging to John's.

Cara nodded. "Yeah, they went out a while back, but they're just friends now. Tiff said Teddy has the best parties in town though, so she didn't want to burn any bridges."

John's suspicions mounted. He'd thought he'd seen a woman in the parking deck. And the dark brunette he'd seen at Teddy's watching him from the foyer was the same one in the picture on the wall. So, Tiffany Maylor had been at Teddy's when they were there.

Had she heard them asking questions? Had she shot at them when they'd gone down to the parking deck?

"Does Tiffany own a gun?" John asked.

Cara's eyes twitched. "You really should talk to Tiffany."

"Does she own a gun?" he asked again.

Tiffany shrugged. "Yeah, a pistol. She said she bought it for protection."

"What kind was it?"

"I don't know," Cara said. "I hate guns myself and made her keep it locked in her room."

"Is it there now?"

Anxiety darkened her eyes. "She usually takes it with her when she goes out at night. Tiff says a girl can't be too careful."

John studied her roommate. Maybe Tiffany had told Cara that she had the weapon for protection. Or maybe she'd gotten mad at Honey and decided to get rid of her, then tried to shoot them earlier?

SAM MASSAGED HER TEMPLE as they headed back to the car. "Where to now?"

"Let's go back to Teddy's party and see if Tiffany is still there."

A few minutes later, they rang Teddy's doorbell again. When Teddy answered, the music was still pounding, the party overflowing, booze floating through the room. Teddy's eyes looked bloodshot, and he staggered slightly as he stared up at them.

"What the hell?" Teddy stuttered. "You back to harass me?"

"Do you own a gun, Wexler?" John asked without preamble.

Teddy's eyes flashed with anger. "Look, you got no jurisdiction here, so get lost." He started to shut the door, but John caught it with his hand.

"Maybe not, but I have spoken with the police and we're working on getting a warrant to search your place."

Teddy barked a laugh. "Well, good luck with that."

Again, Teddy reached to shut the door, but John kept it firmly open. Behind him, Sam saw guests starting to stare. "I want to speak to one of your guests. Tiffany Maylor."

Teddy relaxed slightly. "How'd you know she was here?"

"Just get her," John ordered.

Teddy leaned his head back and shouted, "Tiffany, come here, baby."

The guests nearby all turned to watch, then the beautiful brunette he'd seen earlier in the doorway photo wove her way through the throng, a martini in one hand, diamonds glittering on her earlobes and fingers.

With her looks and obvious fortune, she could have easily bought herself the spot on the cheerleading squad.

Sam's heart clenched for Honey. She probably hadn't had a chance in the cutthroat world she'd dreamed of being a part of.

Tiffany's blue eyes crinkled when she spotted them. Teddy must have told her about them.

Had she been the shooter in the parking deck earlier?

Tiffany took a sip of her martini and flung a jeweled hand up on Teddy's shoulder. "What is it, lover boy?"

John grimaced and Sam stiffened. Honey might have

tried to fit into this world, but she wouldn't want any part of it.

"Miss Maylor, I'm John Wise. I'm here investigating the disappearance of Honey Dawson."

Tiffany's bland expression showed disinterest although her fingers tightened on the stem of the martini glass just enough to reveal her discomfort.

"Why don't you step into the hallway?" John suggested. "Unless you want all of your guests to hear our conversation."

She threw a glance over her shoulder and seemed to decide that she wanted the conversation to be private, then stepped into the hallway. Teddy Jr. followed her, and shut the door, then they both leaned against the wall, trying to act as if they were unfazed by the interrogation. But Teddy's blurry eyes twitched with worry, and Tiffany was holding the glass so tightly Sam expected it to shatter.

"Tell us about your relationship to Honey," John said.

"We didn't have a relationship," Tiffany said.

Sam folded her arms across her chest. "That's not what we heard."

Tiffany shrugged. "We were both trying out for the same spot on the Dallas cheerleading squad, but there were other girls at tryouts, too."

"Yeah, but after the cuts, it came down to one spot, and you and Honey vying for that one, didn't it?" John asked.

Tiffany quirked her ruby red lips. "Yeah. So. That's the name of the business."

"Honey was your big rival," John said matter-of-factly. "And you wanted to get rid of her so you could have that spot."

"I didn't have to do anything to Honey to earn that spot," Tiffany purred. "Eventually everyone saw she was a tramp, and I was the high-class girl they wanted for the Cowboys." She rolled her eyes and hitched out her hip, showing off her tanned long legs. "I mean, can you imagine? Honey was a small-town ho who didn't even know her mama and daddy's names. I, on the other hand, come from the Maylor family. Everyone in Texas knows our reputation."

She turned a pointed look toward Sam. "So who do *you* think the team would want representing them?"

Anger mushroomed inside Sam. "Just because Honey didn't grow up with your money and lifestyle doesn't mean that she didn't deserve that spot. Rich girls like you always get what you want because you don't have to work for it." She clenched her hands to keep from slugging the vile girl. "In fact, Honey should have been chosen. She would have been a role model to prove to other young women that they should pursue their dreams and fight for them."

Silence stretched between the four of them at her outburst, but John finally spoke.

"When did you last see Honey?"

Tiffany shrugged, the strap to her camisole falling off one shoulder. "The day she was cut."

"Really?" John asked.

"Yeah, really," Tiffany said with a sharp laugh. "It's not like we hung out in the same circles or anything."

Sam glanced at Teddy, who had clamped his mouth shut, questions mounting in her mind. What if the cheerleading spot wasn't the only thing Tiffany and Honey were competing for? What if a man had come between them?

But who? Teddy?

Even though her roommate said Tiffany and Teddy's relationship had been in the past, Tiffany was hanging all over Teddy as if he belonged to her. What if Tiffany wanted Teddy, but Teddy had wanted Honey?

"Did you and Honey ever hook up?" Sam asked.

Teddy shifted, avoiding her gaze. "No."

John could have been right. If Teddy had wanted Honey and she turned him down yet slept with his father, he might have been angry.

Or if Tiffany perceived Honey as a threat to Teddy's future—and her future with him—maybe she followed Honey and tried to hurt her and the twins. The girl obviously always got what she wanted.

Would she kill to keep her cheerleading spot and Teddy?

JOHN'S HEAD SPUN WITH the growing number of suspects. Honey had traded men like some women traded purses. In spite of Tiffany Maylor's money and looks, she'd obviously worried that she'd lose to her.

"Where were you three nights ago?" John asked.

Tiffany leaned against Teddy. "Right here in town, of course. I can't miss practice."

John frowned. That fact could easily be checked. "What about your gun? Do you have it with you?"

She muttered a low sound, then planted a hand on her hip. "Yeah. It's in my purse."

"Go get it," John said.

"Don't you need to make an arrest or have a warrant for that?" Teddy piped up.

John shot him a challenging look. "Only if she has something to hide."

"I don't," Tiffany said, then twirled around, went inside and came back carrying a small, black patent leather designer clutch. She unsnapped the flap, and started to reach inside, but John held up a warning hand.

"Let me."

She gave him a bored look, and he reached inside, pulled out the .22 and examined it. The gun hadn't been fired recently, meaning she hadn't used it to shoot at them earlier.

"Let me see your hands," John said.

She scowled at him but flicked them up, and he examined them. No signs of powder burns, either.

Not that that meant she or Teddy weren't responsible, just that they hadn't used this gun.

Dammit. He'd hoped to nail her, but nothing was ever easy. Especially this case.

"How about your hands and gun?" he asked Teddy.

"We're done here, Wise. If you want anything else, come back with that warrant."

Teddy grabbed Tiffany's hand and dragged her back inside to the party. Sam glared after them, and he guided her toward the elevator in silence. It was past midnight now, too late to question anyone else. But tomorrow he'd track down Portia Wexler and Reed Tanner and question them. And maybe Detective Arnold would have a lead on Neil Kinney.

"I can't believe this is happening," Sam said as they checked into a nearby hotel. He asked for adjoining rooms, determined to protect her. Her lack of protest indicated the depth of her despair over Honey's disappearance.

The bellman arrived and escorted them to their rooms and John tipped him as he settled their overnight bags inside.

"Are you hungry, Sam?" he asked.

Her gaze looked tortured as she turned to him. "No. I just keep thinking about Honey and her baby boy and wondering where they are."

He glanced at Sam and saw the torment on her face, and his heart pounded. More than anything, he wanted to find Honey and her babies and bring them home safely. And not just for Honey.

He didn't want to disappoint Sam.

She'd been hurt and alone all her life, and he suddenly wanted to be the man who played her hero.

Chapter Fifteen

A heartbeat of silence reverberated through the hotel room as she and John stepped inside the room.

Sam stared at the big empty bed with a pang of loneliness. Plush cream carpeting covered the floors, and the ivory down comforter with thick pillows looked inviting and romantic. Yet the worry knotting her stomach over Honey and her twins made her feel ill.

And desperate for someone to cling to.

John's room was only a few feet away, but he hadn't retreated to it yet. Instead he stood, watching her quietly, his intense protectiveness sending a tingle of awareness—and desire—rippling through her.

"We will find her," he said as if he'd read her troubled thoughts.

Sam turned to him. "We have to, John," she said softly. "Honey is so special."

"Sam, you don't have to keep singing Honey's praises. I understand how close you are, and I'm not passing judgment on her. I want to find out what happened to her and the twins, too."

"Because it's your job," Sam said, tensing. "Not anything personal."

His jaw tightened. "It is personal to me," John said. He lifted her chin with his thumb. "I want to find her for you, Sam, because I think you're pretty damn special yourself."

His gruff admission touched her deep inside and unleashed a yearning to be in his arms. Temptation overcame Sam, and she pressed the palm of her hand to his jaw.

"Thank you, John. You're the most honorable man I've ever known."

Emotions flickered across his face, and he took a step closer to her, so close she inhaled his masculine scent, so close she felt his breath on her cheek, so close she saw hunger flare in his deep brown eyes.

"Sam…"

She leaned into him, wanting more. Wanting his mouth on hers, his hands touching her. "Yes?"

"God, you're sexy."

Sam's eyes widened. No man had ever called her sexy before. "I'm not," she whispered.

A smile curved his mouth, and he traced his finger along the edge of her face, tucking a strand of curls behind her ear. "Yes, you are. Your strength and tenacity and fierce independence are sexy." His mouth parted and he tilted his head sideways. "At least to me."

Sam's heart swelled with emotions, her body tingling with need. Then Sam lowered his head and fused his mouth with hers. She threaded her fingers in his thick hair, pulling him closer as she savored the feel of his lips against hers. His hands trailed down over her shoulders to her waist, then lower to her hips, and he gripped her to him and wedged his leg between her thighs, stroking her with his body and deepening the kiss.

A thousand butterflies took flight in her stomach, titillating sensations fluttering through her as he probed her lips apart with his tongue and made love to her with his mouth.

He backed her toward the wall and pressed her up against it, and Sam moved beneath him, sliding her foot up and down his calf, aching for more. He made a gruff throaty sound as he dragged his mouth from hers, then trailed kisses along her jaw and neck and nibbled at the sensitive skin behind her ear. She clung to him, sighing in contentment when his hand moved to her breast, and he cupped the heavy mound in his palm.

His lips moved lower, nipping at the edges of her blouse and he slowly unbuttoned one button, then the next until her shirt gaped open. She sucked in a sharp breath, wondering what he would think, then his soft murmur of pleasure echoed in the silence, and he traced his tongue downward until he teased her nipple through the thin lace of her bra.

Her nipples stiffened to turgid peaks, aching for his mouth, and she tore at his shirt, silently urging him for more. He inched his fingers to the front clasp of her bra and flipped it open, and her breasts spilled out. Her chest rose as she exhaled a shaky breath, and he paused to stare at her.

"John," she whispered, suddenly self-conscious.

"You're beautiful," he murmured. His gaze met hers, and the raw hunger in his eyes sent a fiery trail of need through her.

She closed her eyes as he lowered his head and tugged one nipple into his mouth. His other hand pulled her closer, then he unzipped her jeans. The rasp of the zipper cut into the tense silence, spiking her excitement more. She wanted them both to be naked, flesh against flesh, skin against skin, bodies joined as one.

She reached for his zipper, but suddenly his cell phone trilled. For a brief moment, she prayed he'd ignore it, and he did. He suckled her other nipple into his mouth and teased her until her legs crumbled, and he had to hold her up.

But the sound of the phone continued to intrude, and she knew he had to answer it.

It might be news about Honey.

JOHN DIDN'T WANT TO STOP. He wanted Sam with every fiber of his being. His sex was hard and throbbing, his heart pounding, his breath coming in shallow, ragged pants.

Who would have thought that practical, caretaker, tough Samantha Corley was a sex siren beneath her sensible clothes? And that bra—it wasn't exactly sensible. No, it was pure sheer lace and so feminine that he wanted to see the panties he had a feeling would match them, and tear them off until there was nothing between him and Sam but bare skin and sweat and hormones.

But his damn phone wouldn't shut up.

And his cop instincts kicked in. Good God, he was working a major case, a woman's life was at stake as well as two babies. And he was mauling Sam and ignoring his duties.

He slowly extricated himself, pulling Sam's shirt back together to cover those voluptuous breasts, regret for taking it so far mingling with disappointment that he couldn't finish.

Sam sank onto the bed with a shaky sigh as he reached for his phone. Dammit, his father.

He started to forget the phone and toss Sam down onto the bed and make love to her. But his father would only keep calling if he ignored him.

And he should slow it down with Sam. He could act on hormones and walk away. But Sam—she deserved better.

Gritting his teeth, he connected the call.

"John, what in the hell took you so long to answer?"

"I'm busy," he said, glancing at Sam who looked dazed and sexy and too damn tempting for any man to resist.

"I called your office and they said that you're in Dallas, that you're with that Corley woman."

John clenched the phone with a white-knuckled grip, gestured to Sam that he'd be right back, then stepped into the adjoining room and pulled the door closed. "Dad, I'm investigating a case. The clues led me here to Dallas."

"This is about that trampy Dawson girl, isn't it?" His father's voice spiked a decibel.

"Dad, she went missing in my town where I'm in charge," John said, his temper rising. "And there are two babies involved, one of which is also missing. What kind of police officer would I be if I didn't investigate this crime?"

His father muttered his disapproval. "So why is that Corley girl with you?"

John's pulse jumped at the way his father made Sam's name sound vile. "Because she's Honey's friend and someone tried to kill her."

"Well, you could have put someone else in charge of her," his father said. "How do you think it looks for you to be gallivanting around the country with a girl whose daddy was known to be a bad cop?"

John glanced at the closed door between him and Sam, remembering the way she'd felt in his arms, the way she'd looked so dazed and sexy and...tempting.

He should keep that door closed.

"I don't give a damn what people think," John muttered.

"Well, you'd better," his father growled. "You and I have both worked too hard to let some woman destroy your future."

Raw anger surged through John. "Sam isn't responsible for what her father may or may not have done. And what can be more important than finding a man who would hurt a woman and her children?"

"Your career, that's what. Now, get this over with and then we'll talk. And remember what I said, don't get involved with that Corley girl. She could ruin you."

John disconnected the call in a fit of rage and turmoil. He had worked hard to earn his reputation and had aspired to move from Butterville and pursue politics. And he knew how the game was played, that Sam might not fit into it.

Still, he wanted her.

But he paced the room, trying to purge his pent-up anger and lust. He did want her, but just for the night. And Sam would want more.

He reached for the door, tempted...

But rationale set in and he stepped back and went to take a cold shower. The door was closed between them. It was better he kept it that way.

SAM CLUTCHED HER SHIRT to her, feeling alone and vulnerable and wondering if John would come back.

Her body was still tingling from his lips and hands, and she wanted more, for John to make love to her.

She stood and walked to the closed door, then hesitated, her nerves kicking in as the reality of why they were here crashed into her consciousness.

Who was on the phone with John? Did he have bad news about Honey?

Hastily she buttoned her blouse, then raised her hand and knocked on the adjoining door. When John opened the door, he'd straightened his own clothing, and wore his professional expression, his gaze not quite meeting her eyes.

"John, is something wrong? Was that call about Honey?"

"No," he said. "It was my father."

Sam frowned at the distance she felt between them.

"Is everything all right?" she asked.

He gave a clipped nod. "He wants me to come to Atlanta to meet some political constituents."

"I see." Did that mean he was planning to leave Butterville soon? If so, she wouldn't see him again.

The thought sent an odd ache through her chest—this might be the only chance she had to be with him. "John," she said softly. "Do you want to come back to my room?"

He finally lifted his head to look at her. A seed of hunger flared bright and hot, but he held back, regret passing across his face. "Get some sleep, Sam. We need to get an early start tomorrow."

Sam stared at him for a long moment, her heart racing. She'd practically asked him to make love to her and he'd turned her down. Why? She sensed he wanted her. His body couldn't have lied.

And if that phone call hadn't interrupted them, they would be in bed. So what had changed?

Hurt and confused, she went to her room and shut

the door between them. But as she crawled in bed and closed her eyes, she dreamed that he would join her.

FATIGUE WEIGHED ON JOHN the next morning. All night he'd been plagued with questions about the case, and fantasies about making love to Sam. He showered and dressed, then knocked on Sam's door. When she answered, she was already dressed, her expression cool.

Damn. He wanted to pull her into his arms and kiss that iciness right out of her. But they had work to do.

The sooner he solved this case, the sooner he could leave Sam and Butterville behind.

They ate breakfast in strained silence, then he drove to the police station and dropped off the bullet casings he'd collected at the parking garage the night before.

"Where to now?" Sam asked, all business.

"To Judge Wexler's house to question his wife."

Sam lapsed into silence again as he drove, and guilt nagged at him. He'd meant to do the noble thing the night before by not taking advantage of her, but judging from the lackluster look in her eyes, he must have hurt her.

Well, hell. He was trying to *protect* her. Not hurt her.

But he was damned however he handled it.

His mood soured as they approached the Wexler property. His father would be in his element dealing with the judge's power and money, but distaste filled John's mouth as he parked in the circular drive, and he and Sam walked up to the house and rang the doorbell. Again, the housekeeper greeted them and showed them inside.

"We need to speak to Mrs. Wexler," John said.

Louisa nodded, and showed them to the living area, then disappeared. A few minutes stretched out, then Portia Wexler appeared draped in diamonds and a designer tennis outfit, a haughty air about her as she strode toward them. Louisa placed a tray of coffee and china cups on the coffee table, and Portia poured a cup and offered it to him. John declined, and so did Sam, so Portia added sweetener then sipped it herself.

John introduced them and explained about his investigation.

Portia offered a fake smile. "Yes, my husband mentioned that you were here yesterday."

John cut to the chase. "The judge said that you knew about his affair with Honey Dawson."

A flicker of resentment sparked Portia's eyes before she masked it. "Yes, that was a mistake. But it didn't last long."

"Did you ever meet Honey?" John asked.

She shook her head. "No, no reason. Teddy broke it off himself, but she came back and tried to milk him for money."

"We heard that Honey broke it off," Sam said.

Portia's eyes turned cold as she faced Sam. "You heard wrong."

"You're aware that Honey had twins," John said.

Portia took another sip of coffee. "She claimed they were Teddy's, but I didn't believe her for a second. She was a gold digger who just wanted money. I wouldn't be surprised if she hadn't gotten pregnant so she could blackmail him, and no telling how many other men, for money."

Sam clenched the chair edge and John laid a hand over hers to keep her from pouncing on Portia.

Barely suppressed rage tinged her voice when she spoke. "Judge Wexler said that he wanted to raise the twins as his."

Portia flicked her hand up in a dismissive gesture. "Yes, well, Teddy has a soft spot for children, and if he did turn out to be their father, we agreed to raise them."

"But you still don't think the twins are your husband's children?" Sam asked.

"No," Portia said with an air of confidence. "The timing was off. And after all, men were a dime a dozen to Honey."

"Where were you four nights ago?" John asked.

Portia traced her finger over the edge of her delicate china cup. "Having dinner with my son Teddy."

"So if you don't think your husband fathered the babies," Sam said, "then who did?"

"Like I said, Honey had a lot of men. Before she seduced my husband, she was apparently involved with someone named Reed Tanner."

"How do you know Tanner?" John asked.

Portia scoffed. "The maniac showed up here asking about Honey and the babies. And then he assaulted my son, Teddy. If you ask me, he's a menace to society and should be locked up."

John considered her answer. Reed Tanner's name kept popping up. John definitely needed to talk to him. If Tanner was the father of those babies, maybe Teddy and Portia were telling the truth. Maybe Tanner had come after Honey and the twins."

"If he hurt Honey," John said, "why would he be asking you and Teddy about her?"

"I have no idea," Portia said. "Maybe she faked being hurt, and dumped the kids so she could go hook up with some other man. I can't see her being a decent mother."

Sam tensed again, her claws protracting as if she were ready to attack.

But Portia's theory held some credence.

What if Honey had been totally freaked out by having children? The responsibility could have overwhelmed her as it obviously had her mother, and she could have dumped one baby on one person, then the other on Sam so she could continue her party lifestyle, maybe even go back and try out for the cheerleading spot again.

THAT GEORGIA COP and Corley broad were asking way too many questions. They had to be stopped.

But first, they had to lead him back to that baby girl. As long as she was out there, she could make trouble for him, could mess up his life.

And nobody was going to do that.

Honey Dawson should have listened to him. Should have done everything he'd said. Should have taken the money and run.

Hell, at least Honey was gone now.

But he had to finish the job so those brats wouldn't come back to haunt him.

Chapter Sixteen

"I can't believe everyone is being so hard on Honey," Sam said as they drove toward Springton to Reed Tanner's family ranch. "I know she liked men, but everyone just wants to throw the blame on someone else."

John made a sound low in his throat. "Sam, that's generally the way police work goes. It's rare for a suspect to admit up front that he's a killer or criminal. They try to throw off the police."

"Well, it's not fair."

John squeezed her hand. "You see a lot of unfairness in your work, Sam. How do you deal with it?"

She bit her lip. "I try to get justice for the kids. That's all I can do."

"I know," John said, frustration wearing on him. "Sometimes, though, it doesn't feel like enough."

She sighed and turned to look out the window as they drove to Springton.

Immediately, John noted the differences between the Wexler Ranch and Tanner's. Instead of a mini-presidential mansion, Tanner's house was light blue with fading paint. No expensive white wood fencing, either. Barbed wire roped off the land and no animals were in sight. The property looked run-down and deserted. Weeds choked the land, flowerbeds badly needed tending, and a rusted pickup truck had been left in the middle of a field. He spotted a cattle grate in the gravel drive with a wrought-iron entrance sign with the name "Double Kay Ranch" painted on it. More barbed wire fencing stretched around the pastures, and a weathered, whitewashed barn with a corral sat to the side.

He pulled down the drive and parked. "Let me lead the questions here, Sam. We don't know if Tanner is being framed by the Wexlers or if he is dangerous like they suggested."

"Fine," Sam said, that wall he'd erected the night before standing like a mountain between them.

They climbed out and walked up the steps to the porch, but before he could knock, the door opened and a tall broad-shouldered man walked out.

No servants here. And not a friendly greeting at all.

The movement he'd detected inside when he'd parked? Apparently Tanner had been watching for visitors, on the alert. Defensive.

Which raised John's suspicions. And judging from the expression on his face, Tanner had pegged him for a cop, and he didn't like or trust the law.

The man obviously had something to hide.

"Reed Tanner?" John asked.

"Yes."

"John Wise. Samantha Corley. We need to ask you a few questions."

"You're cops?"

"I am." John flashed his badge. "Ms. Corley works as a children's advocate."

Tanner's throat tightened. A sign he was nervous in John's book.

He had to push for more. "As I understand it, you don't live in this area any longer."

"Right. I moved about a year ago. To San Francisco."

John pressed his lips together and nodded slightly, maintaining a cool expression. "And what brings you back?"

Tanner tensed his shoulders, a movement so small he probably didn't even realize he'd made it, but a telltale sign of stress.

"I'm tying up some loose ends."

John swallowed back his irritation. "Loose ends? Explain."

Tanner glanced over the flat expanse of pasture as if he was trying to organize his thoughts. The real estate sign swung slightly in the breeze. "I'm putting my mother's ranch on the market."

"You said you moved a year ago. It's taken that long to decide to do this?"

A lone minute passed while Tanner mentally put together his story, a ploy John had seen before.

"My mother's death was very traumatic," Tanner said. "I've needed time to get used to the idea."

John stifled any emotion he might feel for the guy. Sentiment had no place in a criminal investigation.

But Sam spoke up, in a low heartfelt voice. "I'm sorry for your loss."

Reed nodded his sincere thanks.

John wasn't so sympathetic. "I hear you and Honey Dawson had a relationship before you left Texas."

"We did."

"Were you aware that she gave birth to twins a few months ago?"

Another shuddered look as if he intended to head John off at the pass. "And you're wondering if they're mine?"

John arched a brow. "Are they?"

"I don't know."

"But you know about the babies." It wasn't a question, but a statement. "Honey contacted you about them?"

Tanner paused, a silent debate on how to answer warring in his eyes. Answering yes would only lead to more questions. Answering no would foster suspicion about how he'd learned about the twins. "I got a note from Honey."

Sam piped up. "You haven't seen her? Talked to her?"

"No."

John traded a look with Sam. He didn't buy it. "What did the note say?"

"That she had twins. I don't remember the rest."

"I'll bet."

"We have located one of the children."

A slight twitch of Tanner's eyes revealed his interest. "Where is she? Where did you find her?"

"How did you know the baby we've located is a girl?"

"Just a lucky guess."

"Where is the other baby, Tanner?"

"I don't know."

"You don't know, or you're not telling?" John asked.

Sam peered past him as if trying to see in the front window of the house.

"How did you know I was in town?" Tanner asked.

"We talked to a friend of yours."

Tanner narrowed his eyes. "A friend? What friend?"

"Theodore Wexler Junior. It seems the two of you had a reunion at his condo last night."

"A reunion? That's what he called it?"

"You did a number on his nose. And I can see he got a few licks in, too."

Reed's hand shifted as if he had to resist the urge to bring his hand to the bruise under his eye. "If you want to look at someone who could hurt Honey, Teddy Junior would be a good place to start. Not here."

"Interesting. He said you might tell us that."

"Gee, if a Wexler said it, then you know it has to be true. What else did he say?"

"He said the two of you talked about Honey and her babies last night at the party. He said that you went into a jealous rage."

Reed's gaze twisted back to the house for a second as if he was hiding something inside. Or someone.

"I have no reason to be jealous."

"Really? That's not what he said. He told us you've had it in for him ever since he beat you out for quarterback in high school. He said your animosity extends to his father."

Tanner remained silent, the wheels obviously turning in his head. He knew they were talking about the judge.

John continued, "And his stepmother told us you visited her. She's confirmed everything he said."

"So why are you here? To arrest me?" Tanner asked.

"We'd like to take a look inside the house."

"Get a warrant."

Dammit. John wasn't surprised at his response, but he didn't like it. "You're making yourself look guilty of everything Teddy Wexler Junior accused."

"You've given me no way around that."

"Just tell us the truth," Sam said in a low, soothing voice. "Help us find Honey. Help us find her baby. Please."

Sam's plea seemed to diffuse Tanner's defensive attitude slightly.

"I'm looking for Honey, too. That's the real reason I'm here. I'm worried something has happened to her."

"Why?" John asked. "What prompted your worry?"

A moment of silence, then Tanner answered as if he had no choice. "A few days ago, Honey came to my boat in San Francisco, but she left before I arrived. I haven't been able to find any sign of her since."

"So you saw her a few days ago?" John said in a hard voice.

Tanner looked him square in the eye. "No. I never saw her. I haven't seen her since I left the Dallas area a year ago. I'm looking for her, too."

"So you were in San Francisco?"

"Yes. I flew here two days ago."

John still didn't trust him. He could have chased Honey to Atlanta. "And you went nowhere else in between?"

"No. I took a flight straight here."

"Can anyone confirm that?"

Tanner dug out his wallet and pulled his baggage claim ticket and handed it to him. "I filed a report with the San Francisco police the day before I left, and I hired a private investigator to help look for Honey. She was with me on the flight."

So both Wexler and Tanner claimed they'd hired private investigators. "What's her name? Can we talk to her?"

"J. R. Dionne. But she's not here at the moment. I can have her call you if you give me a number."

John narrowed his eyes, then thrust the baggage claim back into Tanner's hands. "If you've been looking for Honey, tell me what you've found?"

"Judge Teddy Wexler thinks the babies are his. He says he wants to raise them. And he has lawyers looking for Honey."

Hearing Tanner's theory about the judge didn't surprise John in the least. He didn't like anything about the snotty judge. "Is there anyone else you can think of who might want to hurt Honey?"

Tanner rubbed the back of his neck. "Neil Kinney."

John clenched his teeth. The stalker's name again. He needed to see just how much this man knew. "What is his involvement with Honey?"

"One-sided. He started by peeping in her windows and following her everywhere she went. He moved on to rifling through her underwear drawer. He did time for burglary for that one."

Had Tanner tracked him down? "Where is he now?"

"Here. He was following us yesterday. He drives a green pickup with a big dent in the hood."

John didn't know if Tanner was telling the truth or trying to deflect suspicion from himself. But he sure as hell had a reason to suspect Kinney.

"Tell me one thing," Tanner said.

John focused intently on him, as did Sam, but as they'd discussed in the car, he took the lead. "What?"

"The baby girl. Is she okay? Is she safe?"

Genuine concern tinged the man's voice. This time Sam answered.

"Yes," Samantha said. "And I can assure you, she'll stay that way."

Tanner looked down at the dirty gravel under his feet.

"Thanks."

John sighed. Whether or not Tanner was the father of the babies, he seemed relieved that little girl was okay.

Obviously Tanner was another one of the men Honey had loved and left. And if Tanner really cared about the babies, had he hired a private investigator to get them back? Had Honey been running from him, Wexler or Kinney?

His gut impression told him that Tanner and Honey would have been more of a match than she and the judge. Of course, Honey might have set her sights higher on the Wexler money, and if Tanner actually cared about her or the babies and she'd chosen Wexler over him, that could have pissed him off.

And a pissed-off man was dangerous, especially one where paternity issues were in question. Judge Wexler had claimed he'd wanted to raise the babies as his own.

What if Tanner wanted the twins and knew that Wexler could buy them? He apparently didn't have the wealth or power to compete with a man like that. He could have confronted Honey and things had gone sour....

His cell phone buzzed, and he checked the number. The Dallas Police Department. "I need to take this," he said, then handed Tanner his business card and headed toward the car.

Sam followed, worrying her bottom lip with her teeth. He connected the call as he settled in the driver's seat. "Wise."

"Wise, it's Detective Arnold. Listen, we found Kinney's place. You might want to get over here and take a look."

The man's tone of voice raised the hair on the back of John's neck. He memorized the address and sped down the graveled drive from the Double Kay toward Dallas, wondering what the detective had found and hoping it led them closer to Honey.

"THAT WAS DETECTIVE ARNOLD," John said as they drove away from the Tanner ranch. "They found Neil Kinney's place and want me to come by."

"Was Kinney home?" Sam asked.

"I don't know. That's all he said." He turned on the highway leading away from Springton back toward Dallas. "What did you think of Tanner?"

"I don't know what to make of him," Sam said, replaying the scene at his house in her mind. "Reed Tanner certainly seemed more Honey's type than Judge Wexler, but Honey had wanted her dreams and might have thought the judge could help her reach them.

"I think Reed Tanner was hiding something," Sam admitted. "But also that he might have cared for Honey. He sounded sincerely worried about the babies."

"Maybe," John grunted. "He definitely knew more than he admitted. I have a feeling he knows where that baby boy is."

Sam stewed over that possibility. "Maybe he does. Maybe he's trying to keep him safe like we're doing Emmie."

"Then why not cooperate?" John asked.

"I don't know." Sam lapsed into silence as they finished the drive. Hopefully Detective Arnold had answers.

Forty-five minutes later, they arrived at Neil Kinney's. He lived on the outskirts of Dallas in a small rental house. Patches of dirt and brittle grass dotted the lawn, the paint was chipping off and two of the shutters were hanging at odd angles.

A police car and CSI unit were parked in the narrow driveway, and John spun in behind them. Together they walked up the sidewalk and a police officer greeted him, then led them into the house. Sam noted the plaid brown sofa, faux leather recliner, small TV and a half dozen girlie magazines scattered on the coffee table.

Detective Arnold met them at the door to the bedroom, a grave expression on his face. Sam tensed, sensing he had bad news.

"I thought you'd like to see what we found," he said to John.

John nodded and they followed him inside. Sam's stomach turned at the sight.

Dozens of photos of Honey covered one wall, candids of her at her apartment, at cheerleading tryouts, on dates with other men, shots of her and Reed Tanner, of her and Judge Wexler, of Honey pregnant at a store shopping for baby items, of Honey and the twins.

Photos that were recent.

"He's been stalking her again," Detective Arnold said. He gestured to the dresser where a manila envelope lay. Another picture sat on the dresser, this one of Honey when she was in high school—a picture of her and Sam together.

Detective Arnold showed them a photo of Neil Kinney—a redheaded man with freckles. Then he pointed to a small sheet of paper. "He had your address, Miss Corley. Neil Kinney knew you and Honey were friends, and he found out where you lived."

Sam's lungs constricted. Kinney could have followed Honey to Georgia and to her place. Kinney could have hurt Honey and now he wanted to hurt her babies. And if he'd come back to Dallas, he could have been following them and shot at them in Teddy Wexler's parking deck.

"You have to find this sick son of a bitch," John muttered. He moved closer to Sam in a protective stance. "And this time when we catch him, he's going to jail and he won't get out."

JOHN WAS SEETHING AS HE and Sam drove away from Kinney's house. He had to find the bastard and lock him up before he hurt Sam.

Evening was falling, the long deserted road he'd taken almost eerie. Suddenly a truck raced up behind him, the headlights blinding, then screeched around them and slammed into his side.

Sam shrieked, and John clutched the steering wheel with a steely grip, trying to maintain control, but the truck rammed the side of the rental car again and sent them bouncing off the road. He braked and the car skidded into a light post, glass shattering on the driver's side and pelting him as the air bags exploded. Metal scrunched as the front bumper folded, and he ripped away his air bag, then reached sideways to see if Sam was all right.

But the door swung open, and suddenly a red-haired man tried to drag Sam from the car.

Dammit, it was Neil Kinney.

Chapter Seventeen

Sam screamed and pushed at Neil Kinney, trying to escape, but he jerked her arm and yanked her to the ground. John reached for his weapon, drew it and shoved at his door to open it. He cursed as the door stuck, then kicked it again and jumped out.

"Stop or I'll shoot!"

Kinney was tall and obviously stronger than he looked, and pulled Sam toward a green pickup truck. But she clawed and kicked at him, and John was afraid to shoot, afraid he'd hit her. Adrenaline surged through him, and he ran after Kinney and attacked him, knocking them all to the ground.

Sam screamed again, and Kinney lost his hold on her, grunting from the impact of John's body slamming into him. Sam pushed to her hands and knees and crawled to the side of the street.

Fury raged through John, and he punched Kinney with his fist, but Kinney swung his fist up and connected with John's nose. John cursed, and they rolled, trading punches, but his rage enhanced his strength, and he overpowered Kinney, gave him a hard right, then rolled him to his back and straddled him.

Kinney bucked, but John shoved his gun in his face. "We know who you are, Kinney."

Kinney's eyes widened, his pale skin glowing white in the headlights. "Wait, please don't shoot me."

Out of the corner of his eyes, John saw Sam shove her tangled hair from her face and push to her feet.

"Are you all right, Sam?"

"Yes," she said in a shaky voice.

John turned back to Kinney, tightening his grip on Kinney's arm as he kept his gun aimed at his head. "Where's Honey Dawson?"

Kinney's breath wheezed out. "I don't know," he said. "That's why I stopped you." He jerked his eyes toward Sam. "You're her friend. I recognized you from Honey's pictures, so I figured you could lead me to her."

"You assaulted us with your vehicle and tried to kidnap Sam," John snarled. "You're going to pay for that, you bastard."

"You don't understand," Kinney wailed. "I love Honey. She disappeared a few days ago, and I was worried about her, so I've been trying to find her."

"I've heard that story from a few other people in this town," John said. "I also know that you stalked Honey, broke into her apartment and stole her underwear."

"I went to jail for that," Kinney said. "I served my time. And when I got out I wanted to apologize to Honey, make sure she knows I love her, that I'd never hurt her. Never."

Sam moved over to stand beside them, and crossed her arms. "You stalked her again, and took pictures of her. You even have a picture of me and had my address in your apartment."

"You were watching the police and us there, weren't you?" John asked.

Kinney bobbed his freckled face up and down. "Yes, but I already explained the reason."

"I don't believe you. This is what I think happened," John said through gritted teeth. It was all he could do not to kill the bastard for trying to hurt Sam.

"You thought you loved Honey, and you were jealous when you realized she'd been with other men. Those pictures of her with them tormented you. You couldn't stand the thought of her having another man's baby. If you couldn't have her, no one could."

"She was mine," Kinney shouted. "She *was*."

John's jaw ached from clenching it. He wanted to beat the sick man into a bloody pulp. "That's right, you thought you owned her, so when she tried to leave, you came after her. You caught up with Honey in Georgia and followed her to Sam's, then attacked Honey."

Kinney twitched. "No, that's not what happened. I've never been to Georgia."

John gripped Kinney by the collar of his shirt and shook him. "You're lying. You and Honey fought and when she tried to escape, you attacked her. Is she dead or alive, Kinney? Did you kill her and dump her body somewhere in the mountains or the river?"

"No!" Kinney cried. "I didn't hurt her. I didn't go to Georgia. I swear." Kinney angled his head toward Sam. "Do you know where she is? Is she okay?"

"If I knew, I wouldn't tell you," Sam said. "You're sick, Mr. Kinney, you need help."

"Sam, call Detective Arnold," John said. "Tell him we have Kinney. Maybe a night in jail will persuade this bastard to tell us the truth."

"Think about it," Kinney cried. "If I knew where Honey was, why would I have tried to take you, Sam?"

SAM WAS SHAKING AS Detective Arnold arrived and took Neil Kinney into custody. Even as the detective hand-cuffed him and shoved him into the back of the squad car, Kinney continued to deny that he had hurt Honey and ranted that he loved her and would never harm her.

Sam didn't know what to think or who to believe. Her head was swirling with questions, suspects and worry.

John phoned and arranged for a tow truck to haul the rental car to the repair shop, and one of the uniformed officers drove them back to their hotel. When they arrived, John pulled her close to him as if he thought someone else might try to grab her again.

He remained gruff and silent, jaw rigid, anger radiating off him as he unlocked her room. He pressed his hand to the small of her back and ushered her inside, scanning the hallway and room as they entered. With a raised finger, he gestured her to be quiet and he rushed through both rooms checking them as if he expected to find an intruder.

Her nerves skittered. If he still thought someone was out to get her, then he must think Kinney was innocent.

He returned from the adjoining room, stopped in the doorway, then his dark eyes met hers. He stood rigid, but an odd look flickered in his eyes—anger? Possessiveness? Fear?

Desire?

Her heart fluttered, and her chest ached as her own needs surfaced. She wanted to be held, touched, cared for…loved.

To forget that Kinney's hands had touched her, that he could have done God knows what if John hadn't saved her. To forget that Honey was still missing and might be dead.

That her little baby boy was missing, too, and if anything had happened to him...

When Kinney had grabbed her, déjà vu had struck and she'd relived the horror of her parents' murder. Of the man who'd shot them grabbing her.

She'd fought back, had bitten the man's leg, and that mark had helped the police catch their murderer and send him to jail. But she'd had nightmares ever since.

"Sam?"

She inhaled sharply to stem the emotions churning through her. "What?"

"Are you really all right? Did he hurt you?"

His gruffly spoken words touched her, and she nodded, although she couldn't speak.

His breath hissed out, and suddenly he moved toward her, tension rippling between them, then he pulled her into his arms.

"God, Sam, I thought he was going to hurt you. I...didn't think I could stand that."

Sam sighed and leaned into his hard chest, then curled her hands against him. She'd always felt tough, a tomboy, a fighter and survivor, one who stood alone and wanted no one else.

But next to John's big, muscular frame and height, she felt small and vulnerable and willing to let him take up the slack, as if leaning on him didn't mean she was weak or giving up herself. As if he understood her and liked what he saw.

As if he wanted her for her.

The silence stretched as he held her, and she clung to him, his heart beating beneath her cheek. Desperate to be nearer to him, she pressed a kiss against his neck, inhaling his erotic scent as her lips met the salty skin at his throat.

A sigh escaped him, then he dropped a kiss into her hair. The gesture was so seductive and sweet, the low sound in his throat so hungry that heat flooded her, emboldening her, and she looked up into his eyes.

Desire flared hot and potent, his raw need triggering her own, and she traced her hand over his chest, then lower to tease his stomach, feathering one finger over his zipper.

"Sam?"

"Shh," she whispered, then stood on tiptoe and pressed her lips to his. This time, instead of turning away, he fused his mouth with hers and emitted a guttural groan that sent her heart racing.

The barriers between them fell away in a heated instant, and suddenly their hands and mouths were everywhere. He backed her up to the bed and tore at her clothes, and she returned the favor.

One hungry kiss led to another. Their tongues mated in a dance of love and intimacy that she'd felt with no other man, the erotic noises from his throat echoing in the silence between them. As they fell onto the bed in a frenzy of tongue lashes and caresses, her body felt as if it might explode with the pleasure.

Leaning over her, he paused and raked his gaze over her. Her body tingled as she lay sprawled on the sheets, her soft whispers urging him on as he trailed kisses along her neck, suckled her breasts, then climbed above her and teased her with his hard, throbbing length.

He was huge, masculine perfection at its peak, and she parted her legs, aching to feel him inside her. He stroked her tender bud until she cried out and erotic sensations rocked through her, then he settled himself between her thighs. He reached into his jeans on the foot of the bed, rolled on a condom, and thrust into her.

She gasped at the swift point of entry and pain, but sucked in her breath and savored the sensations that flooded her in its wake. John paused, cushioning her hips with his hands as he searched her eyes. "Sam? I'm your first. Why?"

She cupped his face with her hands. "Because I want you, John," she whispered. Her heart thudded. He couldn't stop now. Couldn't leave her like this, so needy and desperate and hungry, and wanting him deep in her body.

His eyes darkened, a look of primal need on his face, then he tilted her hips up and thrust inside her again, this time filling her to the core. Sam closed her eyes and cried out as sensation after sensation overcame her.

Colors danced before her eyes, and love for John made her heart swell.

JOHN'S BREATH ESCAPED in ragged pants as his climax rocked through him. He'd had sex before, enough in his day to know what was good and what wasn't, enough to know that none had ever torn him up inside and exhilarated him at the same time.

Not wanting to crush Sam, John encircled her in his arms and rolled sideways to cradle her in his embrace, breathing deeply to gain control as the aftermath of their lovemaking slowly dissipated.

But that aftermath left him even more confused. Normally sex was sex.

But this was sex with Sam.

Sam who was a tomboy, a friend, a woman he'd have to leave soon.

Sam, a woman who was a virgin, for God's sakes.

He heaved another breath, tucked her into his arms, his chest swelling at her purr of satisfaction. Yet his mind jumped onto a roller coaster of emotions and questions.

Insecurities set in. Had he really satisfied her?

Hell, he never doubted himself.

Had she read more into the sex than he'd intended? His thoughts ping-ponged. Of course she had.

But he would hurt her in the end when he left Butterville.

Still, she clutched his chest, and her hair tickled his neck as she cuddled into his arms, and he relented and kissed her again. She felt so…right.

For tonight, he'd hold her and let them both pretend that things between them could last.

Tomorrow when morning came, they'd have to return to business. And they couldn't make love again.

SAM DREAMED OF HAPPY TIMES, of being loved and held and having a man by her side. Dreams she'd never had before.

But other dreams intruded. The nightmare of her parents' murder. The years of sleepless nights afterward. The horror of the gossip that had haunted her as she'd grown older.

The fact that the only friend who'd understood and cared for her was Honey.

And now John…

Hours later, she jerked awake to the sound of her cell phone ringing and felt John's arms still around her, his breath on her neck. God, she loved him.

Could John possibly care for her, or had he given in to baser needs because they'd been thrown together on this case?

Her phone buzzed again from her purse, and she eased out of John's arms, climbed naked from the bed and hurried to retrieve it. What if it was Miss Mazie and something was wrong with Emmie?

Her chest constricted, and she glanced at the number. An unknown.

With all that was happening, she quickly connected the call. "Hello."

"If you want to see Honey Dawson alive, then go back to Georgia. You'll receive further instructions then."

The voice sounded electronic, as if it had been altered through a machine. "Wait! How do I know you'll tell me where Honey is?"

"You don't," the voice said. "But if you want to see her alive, you'll do what I said and wait for the call."

Sam's heart pounded, and she ran to wake up John.

Chapter Eighteen

Sam's hands shook as she punched in Miss Mazie's number. She had to make sure Emmie was safe.

Thankfully, Miss Mazie answered and assured her they were both fine.

"Give me the phone," John said. He spoke to the older woman, then asked to speak to his deputy. "You're staying around the clock, aren't you?"

"Yes," Deputy Floyd said, "everything's fine."

"Good, keep it that way. We received a call from the kidnapper and are on the first flight out."

Sam was already packing, and he ended the call, then went to throw his own duffel bag together. They booked the early morning flight, the tension mounting between them during the flight and as they landed. John hadn't spoken about the night they'd spent together and she didn't know how to read him.

At least he hadn't apologized or said their lovemaking was a mistake.

Her body still ached for him, the memory of his touches so sweet and blissful that she wanted to be with him again, wished they could have stayed in bed all day and kissed and loved each other again and again and again.

But Honey and Emmie needed her.

She clenched her phone, hoping to hear from the kidnapper with more instructions as they found John's SUV at the airport and rode back to Butterville. The fall leaves were turning beautiful colors, the majestic view of the mountains radiant. It was a gorgeous day.

Sam only hoped that Honey's kidnapper hadn't lied and that she was still alive.

JOHN WAS SICK OF THIS GAME. He had checked the flight on the way to see if any of their suspects were on board, but found nothing.

As soon as they arrived at the police station, he organized a county wide search and called in a county planner who brought in topical maps of the area to help pinpoint any deserted buildings, houses or cabins that they hadn't searched previously. Dwayne Hicks showed up, eager to help and acting anxious. Sam's silence disturbed him. He wanted to comfort her, but he hadn't broached the subject of their sexual interlude and now wasn't the time.

Sam's phone buzzed, and she stepped into the hall to answer. He studied her movements as she paced, then saw her start down the hall. The hair on the back of his neck prickled, and he hurried toward her and caught her just before she stepped outside.

"What in the hell are you doing?" he asked.

She turned panicked eyes toward him. "He called, John, and he said Honey is alive."

John exhaled. "Where is she?"

"He asked me to meet him."

Rage sizzled through him. "And you were going *alone?*"

She clamped her teeth over her bottom lip. "He said if I didn't, he'd kill her."

John hissed and gripped her firmly by the arms. "Sam, don't you see—this is a trap. He might be lying about Honey being alive just to get you alone so he can kill you." His voice cracked. "And he'll try to force you to tell him where the baby is first."

"Then he'd have to kill me because I'd never do that," Sam said emphatically.

He took a deep breath to control his rage. "That's why you're not going alone."

Sam tried to pull away. "But John—"

"Sam, you are not going to fall into his trap. I want you alive."

"And I want to save Honey."

God, the woman was so damn stubborn. "Then trust me," he growled. "And let's do this together."

Fear clouded her expression, and he wanted to pull her into his arms again, but time was of the essence. "Where did he ask you to meet him?"

Sam's sigh sounded torn. "At the old orphanage where Honey and I met." She clutched his arm. "I should have thought of it sooner."

"Shh," he said quietly. "Now, this is what we'll do. You'll drive and I'll hide in the back."

She studied him for a long moment, then quietly agreed. He hurried to get the keys for an unmarked police car, then they rushed to the car.

MEMORIES OF THE ORPHANAGE bombarded Sam as she drove from town and wound around the mountain. The first night she'd spent at the orphanage after her parents were murdered, she'd been in shock, terrified of the haunted-looking old mansion, and afraid of the dark.

Then Honey had come and crawled in bed beside her.

Fall leaves fluttered to the ground, the wind scattering them along the mountain road as she climbed the ridge. The orphanage looked like a castle, the stone pillars giving it an eerie, ominous, cold feeling. Her heart began to pound as she relived other bad memories there, the day Honey had been taken to Miss Mazie's and she'd been left alone.

Courage and determination fortified her. She had to be strong and save Honey today.

From the backseat floor where John had hidden, he spoke in a low voice. "Park near the building beneath some trees so I can sneak out."

"Got it." She bounced over the graveled drive, then pulled beneath a cluster of oaks. Hopefully the spidery trees would help shield John from sight.

"Don't do anything rash, Sam," John said.

"I won't." Her instincts on alert, she climbed out and scanned the woods and sides of the building but saw nothing. The wind whipped her hair around her face, and dry leaves crunched beneath her feet as she crept up to the entrance.

Stomach knotting, she reached for the heavy wooden door, gripped the steel handle, then slipped inside. The building had been deserted for years, and it showed. Cobwebs draped the corners and ancient light fixtures, the place was icy cold from lack of heat, and darkness shrouded the interior, the scent of decay, dust and mold hanging heavy in the thick air.

The screech of bats and mice skittering in the attic echoed off the concrete walls as she climbed the steps to the dormlike sleeping quarters of the orphanage. Her foot hit a piece of torn carpeting, and she nearly tripped, but she gripped the stone wall, its rough cold texture sickeningly familiar.

Another sound reverberated through the corridors, and she hesitated, wishing John was beside her.

He's close by, she reminded herself. *He won't let anything happen to you.*

Besides, she had to take the chance.

The odd noise sounded again—a low cry. Someone whimpering.

Adrenaline shot through her, and she rushed the rest of the way up the steps, then down the dark hallway, searching the corners for Honey's attacker, then heard the noise again. A cry.

Honey's.

She picked up her pace and ran to the end of the hall, then swung inside and paused to search the shadows. Honey was lying on one of the old cots, her feet and arms bound, her mouth gagged.

But she was alive.

Alive and hurt and crying.

Sam ran toward her, then dropped to her knees and hugged her, searching her face for injuries. "Oh God, Honey, I've been looking everywhere for you. I thought …you were dead."

Honey moaned and jerked at her bindings, and Sam pulled the gag from her mouth.

"Sam, watch out," Honey cried.

Sam spun around, but a man's hard, cold hand connected with her jaw, and she fell backward against Honey, dizzy and disoriented.

JOHN SLIPPED THROUGH the trees and bushes and found a side window, wrapped his jacket around his hand and punched out the glass. He crawled through the opening, then crept through the dark, listening for sounds to alert him where Sam was.

Footsteps on the staircase told him Sam was upstairs, and more footsteps indicated Honey's attacker had followed Sam. He inched his way up the back staircase and paused, then heard a groan and voices.

"You can't kill us," Sam said. "The police will find you."

John slid his gun from the holster, and inched down the corridor toward the voices, praying he made it in time.

"Please," he heard Sam say. "Why are you doing this?"

"Tell me where that damn baby is," the man growled, "or I'll finish you both off right now."

John's heart raced at the fear in Sam's voice, and he hurried toward the dark room, then crept into the entrance and aimed his gun at the ready. The room was filled with shadows, but he instantly sized up the situation. Honey lay bound, gagged and bleeding on a cot, Sam beside her, Teddy Jr. gripping her around the neck with a knife blade inches from her carotid artery.

"Drop it, Wexler," John said through clenched teeth. "It's over."

Even in the dim light, John could see that Wexler's face paled. "You bitch," he snarled. "I told you to come alone."

"You're crazy, Wexler," John said. "You won't get away with this."

Teddy tightened his grip on Sam, and she winced in pain. The bastard was choking her.

"Don't hurt her, Teddy," Honey pleaded. "Please, it's me you want, not Sam."

"They have to die and so do you," Teddy said, a crazed tone to his voice. "I've gone too far now to stop."

John spoke calmly, hoping to diffuse the situation. "That's not true, Teddy. You haven't killed anyone yet. We can strike a deal, you'll get a plea bargain."

"No," Teddy said. "I can't go to jail. My father would disown me."

The son of a bitch was still worried about his damn money. "You are going to jail," John said. "Either that, or I'll shoot you here and you won't make it to the hospital."

Teddy shook his head wildly, then suddenly Sam brought her elbow up and slammed it into Teddy's groin. He grunted in pain, dropped the knife, doubled over and fell to the floor scrambling for the weapon.

Sam tried to kick the knife away, and John fired. The bullet pierced Teddy's shoulder, but he clenched the knife in his other hand and jabbed it at John as he lurched toward him.

The knife stabbed John's thigh, and blood spurted out. Sam screamed, and John slammed the butt of his gun against Teddy's temple.

The man groaned and fell backward, dazed, then unconscious.

"John," Sam cried. "You're bleeding."

He pressed a hand to his thigh, felt the blood trickling, but ignored it and handcuffed Teddy to the old furnace. "Are you okay, Sam?"

"Yes, but you need a hospital."

"Untie Honey and I'll call it in," John said.

Sam gave him a teary look, then turned to her friend and began to try to free her. Tears streaked Honey's dirty cheeks, but she was fighting to undo her bindings.

John glared at Wexler as he called for an ambulance. He wanted to kill the bastard for trying to hurt Sam.

But jail would be worse for a man like Teddy Jr. He'd love to see the judge's face when he saw his son being carted off to prison for attempted murder.

"SAM," HONEY WHISPERED hoarsely. "Oh God, Sam, I can't believe you're here."

Honey collapsed into Sam's arms as soon as she removed the restraints and the two of them hugged and cried.

"God, Honey, I was so scared," Sam said.

"So was I." Honey gasped for a breath. "I thought he was going to kill you. I couldn't have lived with that, Sam."

"And I was afraid for you." They both laughed between their tears. Sam pulled back and cradled Honey's face, examining her. "Are you sure you're all right?"

Honey nodded, swiping at tears with a dirt-stained hand. "I kept thinking he'd kill me but he kept holding out, hoping I'd tell him where my babies were." Panic flashed in her eyes. "You did find Emmie, didn't you, Sam? Please tell me my little girl is all right."

"Yes, I found her," Sam said, wiping at her own eyes. "And she's safe, Honey, I promise."

"Where is she now? I have to see her."

"She's with Miss Mazie and well taken care of. John assigned a guard to protect them around the clock."

Honey's face crumbled again. "Oh, Emmie's with Miss Mazie. I've missed her so much."

"Honey." Sam gripped her friend's hands tightly within her own. "You had another baby, a little boy." Her heart pounded with fear. "Where is he? Did Teddy hurt him?"

"I left him with an old friend of mine in San Francisco, a man named Reed Tanner."

"We met him," Sam said. "When we went to Dallas to track down who'd attacked you."

"He didn't mention that he had the baby." John limped toward them, grabbed one of the old pillowcases and tied it around his leg to stop the bleeding.

"Oh, my God," Honey said. "What if he didn't find Troy or someone got him? I left him on Reed's boat, but I had to leave a note and get out of there because Teddy was on my tail." She clutched John's arm. "We have to call Reed. I have to make sure little Troy is okay."

"Do you know his number?" John asked.

Honey nodded and recited the number, and John punched it in, then handed the phone to Honey just as the sound of a siren wailing reverberated off the mountain.

Honey clenched the phone with a shaky hand. "Reed, this is Honey."

A tense moment of silence passed. "Yes, I'm alive. What about Troy? Did you find him? Is he okay?"

Sam held her breath, and John placed his hand on her shoulder as they waited for his response.

Chapter Nineteen

"He's fine," Honey said, visibly relaxing as she disconnected the call. "Reed is taking care of him. He didn't tell you because he was afraid you would try to take Troy away from him."

The ambulance arrived, along with one of the other deputies, and John ushered them in, grateful they'd found Honey alive and that both the babies were safe.

Wexler stirred from unconsciousness, protesting and screeching as they pushed him toward the squad car and it squealed away.

"I don't need to go to the hospital," Honey protested. "I just want to see my baby girl and hold her. I bet she's grown in the last few days and I've missed it."

John had had doubts about Honey being a good mother, but she obviously loved the little tykes and had done everything she could to protect them.

"You're going to get checked out," Sam told Honey, taking charge. "You're injured and dehydrated, and John needs stitches."

The paramedics loaded Honey and John into the ambulance. Sam followed in the car and met them at the hospital where John received stitches, and Honey was treated for cuts and bruises and received fluids.

Night was falling as they stopped by Miss Mazie's to pick up Emmie. John watched the tearful reunion, a lump in his throat as Honey cradled the baby in her arms.

"Sam, I want you to be my babies' godmother."

Sam traced Emmie's finger over her cheek, then kissed her forehead. "Of course I will, Honey. I love Emmie already. And I know I'll love Troy, too."

John felt oddly out of place, like a third wheel who'd stepped into a happy family's private moment. He drove Sam, Honey and the baby back to Sam's house, resigned to leave them alone, yet already dreading going back to his house.

Just as they made it to Sam's front porch, a woman stepped from behind a cluster of pines. The shiny metal of a gun glinted beneath the moonlight, a gun trained on Honey and Sam. "You shouldn't have come back here, Honey."

SAM FROZE IN SHOCK, and Honey stiffened beside her, hugging the baby to her as Sally Hicks stared them down.

John held up a hand to caution Sally against coming closer. "What are you doing, Sally?"

"Honey called Dwayne," Sally screeched. "She wants him back, that's why she called. But she can't have him, he's mine!"

"Sally, calm down," John said in a low, soothing tone.

"Please," Sam murmured. "You don't want to do this, Sally."

"She dumped him and he came back here, and then he said he loved me. You can't have him now, Honey. You can't." Hysteria made her voice shrill. "I won't let you." She raised the gun to fire, but a truck pulled up and careened to a stop, and Dwayne jumped back, terror-stricken when he spotted his wife with the gun. "Sally, what in the hell are you doing?"

"She can't have you, Dwayne." Sally waved the gun. "I don't know what kind of power she has over men, but I won't let her take you away."

"I'm not trying to get back with Dwayne," Honey said softly. "That's not why I'm here."

"Yes, it is," Sally cried. "You brought that baby here so Dwayne would take care of you."

Sam moved slightly in front of Honey to shield her and Emmie, but Honey pushed Sam aside. "You're always taking care of me, Sam. From now on, I'm taking care of myself and my babies."

"Honey, be careful," John warned. "You don't want to get Emmie hurt."

"Sally, don't do this," Dwayne pleaded. "I love you, not Honey. I want to be with you."

"That's right." Honey clutched the baby protectively. "I did call Dwayne, but only because I needed money. He told me he loved you, Sally, and that he couldn't help me."

Sally's hand shook and she was wavering. "Is that true, Dwayne?"

"Yes, sweetheart." Dwayne inched closer, until he could touch her shoulder. "Put down the gun, and let's go home. We'll make our own baby."

Sally burst into tears, but lowered the gun and dropped it to the ground. "You mean it, Dwayne?"

"Yes, of course I do," he said then pulled her into his arms.

John strode down the steps, picked up the gun,

then reached for his handcuffs. "Sally Hicks, you are under arrest—"

"No." Honey handed Sam the baby, then joined him and Sally. "I'm not pressing charges."

"But Honey," John said. "She tried to kill you."

"I'm not pressing charges." She gave Sally a warm smile. "If I want people around here to forgive me and respect me, then I have to forgive them. Ain't that right, Sally?"

Tears of relief filled Sally's eyes, and she slumped against Dwayne.

"Thanks, Honey." Dwayne hugged his wife in the crook of his arm and herded her back to the car.

Honey sashayed up the steps toward Sam, and they hugged again. John shook his head. For the life of him, he'd never understand women.

Still, he went to open the front door and make sure no other surprises awaited them inside.

"Thank you so much for keeping her safe, Sam." Honey turned to John as they stepped into Sam's cozy, warm house. "And thank you, too, John. I appreciate everything you did to find me and protect Sam and Emmie."

John shrugged. "I was just doing my job." His gaze met Sam's, the memory of their lovemaking taunting him. Last night had been nothing about the case, but about holding and loving Sam.

But the case was over, and now they both had to move on. So he said good-night, then headed to his car to go home alone.

Days Later

"I'M SO NERVOUS MY KNEES are knocking," Honey said as John parked the rental car and she, Sam and her lawyer got out of the car. "What if the judge wins and takes Troy and Emmie away from me?"

"We're not going to let that happen," Sam said, as she scooped a sleeping Emmie from the car seat, although she felt nauseated with worry herself.

"You've got a good case and a support group now, Honey," John said, giving Sam a consoling look over Honey's shoulder.

Sam smiled her thanks, although Honey's lawyer didn't appear to be as confident. He'd warned them about all the people the judge had in his pocket.

The four of them walked inside the law office lobby, Sam holding Emmie close to her chest and allowing Honey to enter first.

"I can't wait to see little Troy again," Honey said, her eyes lighting up with anticipation.

Sam smiled and rubbed Honey's back, anxious to see the baby boy—her godson—too. She still couldn't believe her best friend had twins.

She couldn't lose them.

Then Reed Tanner appeared and engulfed Honey in a hug. "I'm so glad you're okay."

Honey nodded at Reed. Pulling back from the hug, she gave him a little smile. "Thank you for taking care of Troy. I knew I could count on you to keep him safe."

He gave a self-deprecating shrug as if he hadn't been so sure himself. "I had help. Someone I want you to meet."

He nodded to John and her, then frowned at Honey's lawyer tagging along behind.

"Nice to see you, Tanner," John said. He offered his hand.

Reed gripped his hand firmly and shook. "I'm glad circumstances are a little better than the last time we met."

John shifted a nervous glance at the conference room door. "Let's hope circumstances keep improving."

Sam clenched her teeth, aware John was almost as apprehensive about this meeting as she was. Next to him, Honey fidgeted, twining her fingers together and shifting her feet on the marble floor.

Sam rubbed her hand over the pink bundle she held to her shoulder.

Reed grinned despite the tension. "Is this…"

Honey and Sam beamed in tandem. Honey gestured to the baby. "Reed, meet my daughter Emmie."

He stepped around Sam and peered over her shoulder. "Hello, Emmie."

Emmie's little face was delicate and angelic, yet she had a strength about her that Reed obviously recognized and he smiled. Emmie's mouth stretched into a giant yawn.

Reed had been hospitalized after being shot in an effort to protect Troy, and they'd talked to him.

Apparently he'd had quite the ordeal trying to keep Troy safe. No wonder he hadn't trusted them.

They still didn't have the whole story and Sam wanted to know what had happened from the time Honey had left her son in San Francisco to when he'd figured out who was after the baby boy. She couldn't help but wonder what challenges they'd faced. And what further challenges all of them would have to deal with once they walked through that conference room door.

"You have Troy?" Honey asked.

Reed motioned to the conference room. "He's inside, along with a special person I want you to meet."

Reed led Honey, Sam, John and the lawyer into the conference room.

The judge sat at one side of the huge conference table, his lawyers flanking him. Glaring at Honey, he crossed his arms over his chest.

Honey looked straight ahead.

Admiration stirred in Sam's chest. She was proud of Honey for standing up to the judge to protect her children.

Reed focused on the far side of the room and Sam saw a woman in a high-backed conference chair. A clean diaper thrown over one shoulder, she held Troy against her heart and patted his back. When she spotted the group coming toward her, she broke into a tense smile.

Honey made a beeline for her son and the woman, squealing at the sight of Troy and smothering him with kisses.

Reed introduced them. After much ooing and ahhing over Emmie and Honey's tears over being reunited with Troy, Reed slipped an arm around Josie. "If you want to thank someone for taking care of Troy and keeping him safe, Honey, this is who you need to talk to. I couldn't have done it without her—found out who was trying to hurt him *or* taken care of a baby. Hell, I didn't even know I had it in me."

"Thank you." Honey gave Josie a hug. "He's a good guy."

"I know." Josie nodded toward the baby, now lifting his head shakily from her shoulder and looking at all the people in the room with googly eyes. "Do you want to hold him?"

Honey patted her arm and surprised Sam by saying, "You can for now. I can tell you want to. It's okay."

Either Honey's legs were really shaking so badly she was afraid to hold her son, afraid she'd collapse, or she realized that Reed and Josie had grown attached to Troy. Another sign of how much the babies had changed Honey.

Josie mouthed a thank you, tears pooling in her eyes.

Still, Sam knew the hardest part lay ahead. Fighting Judge Wexler.

"Tick, tock. Tick, tock," the judge called out.

The lawyer who'd apparently accompanied Reed checked his watch and stood. "If everyone will take a seat, we need to get started."

They shuffled into seats. Honey placed her baby bag on the chair beside her.

"As you all know," the lawyer droned, "we're here to see if we can reach an agreement about the custody of the children known as Troy James Dawson and Emmie Samantha Dawson. My client has been very patient in this matter, but he is eager to have contact with his twins."

A knock sounded on the door. It opened, and Jimmy stepped inside. "Sorry to interrupt, but I..."

"What are you doing here?" the judge asked in a loud voice.

"Jimmy!" Honey sprang from her seat and catapulted across the room. Even from this angle, Reed could see tears stream down her cheeks. She hugged Jimmy and gave him a big smack on the lips.

The judge scoffed. "This is outrageous. We're in the middle of a meeting here. Sit down."

If Honey noticed the judge, she didn't react. When the kiss ended, she peered into Jimmy's eyes. "Oh, Jimmy. All those nights when I thought I was a goner,

I kept seeing your face. Of all the people I wished I could see one last time before I died, I wanted to see you the most. I have something I need to tell you."

Jimmy lifted a hand. He wiped the tears from her cheek with gentle fingers, then cupped her face as if it was the most precious thing in the world. "What, baby?"

"I love you, Jimmy."

He looked at her, as if he was afraid to believe her words.

"It's true. I know I always said you were my friend, my buddy. But you're more than that. I just didn't see it. I was so stupid."

"You love me?"

"With all my heart. If you'll have me."

"Are you kidding? I've wanted you since the first time I saw you."

"Blah, blah, blah," the judge boomed. "All these hearts and flowers are real nice, but you're wasting my lawyer's time. Do you have any idea how much they charge? For God's sake, sit down."

Honey wrinkled her nose at the judge. Taking Jimmy's hand, she led him to the chair next to hers. She removed the baby bag and set it on the floor.

Jimmy looked over at Reed, and gave him a civil nod.

Reed returned the gesture.

"Now where were we?" the lawyer said.

"We were getting my kids," the judge snapped.

Reed leaned back in his chair and pressed two fingers at his temple as if a headache pounded at the back of his neck.

Sam gripped John's fingers so tightly she felt him shift but he didn't pull away.

Then Reed thrust his chair back from the table and stood.

The judge made a growling sound low in his chest. "What do you think you're doing, Tanner?"

Reed leveled a look on the judge. "The baby needs changing. Do you think you're up to it, judge?"

A muscle twitched in the judge's cheek.

"Didn't think so."

A smile curved John's mouth, and Sam decided she liked Reed Tanner.

Honey stood. "I can—"

Reed held up a hand. "It's okay. I'll get it. One last time?"

Honey gave him an understanding smile. "Knock yourself out."

He held out his hands, and Josie peeled Troy off her shoulder. He gritted his teeth as if still in pain from the bullet he'd taken to his shoulder, then he carried the baby to a small sofa behind Honey and Jimmy. Josie followed with the baby bag.

Sam was so distracted by the scene that she ignored the droning voice of the judge's lawyer protesting as if they were stalling the inevitable.

Reed worked as a team with Josie. She lay down the changing pad, and he placed the baby on top. He took off the dirty diaper while she unfolded a clean one and handed him the package of wipes.

Sam smiled. Apparently Reed and Josie had taken to parenting just as she and John had.

A twinge of pain caught in her chest. Only they looked as if they might end up together, and she wasn't so sure about her and John.

"Oh, my God." Jimmy pushed back his chair and

sprang to his feet. He stepped over to the sofa where Reed and Josie were changing Troy and knelt down next to the baby.

Honey followed. "What is it?"

"For the love of…" The judge exploded. "What's going on around here? Can't we get through a simple meeting?"

Jimmy extended a finger and pointed to a small darkened patch on the baby's left hip. He looked up at Honey and stuttered, as if he couldn't find the words he wanted to say.

Sam and John crowded around them. Sam spoke first, cradling Emmie to her. "It's a birthmark. Emmie has one like that, too. Right in the same spot."

Jimmy looked up at Honey with watery eyes. "And I do, too. Just like my father."

For a moment, the air seemed to leave the room. Reed looked as if he was struggling to pull in a breath, then another. He must have thought the twins were his. "Jimmy is the twins' father."

Josie grinned at him and nodded.

"Sorry, judge," John said, grinning broadly. "It looks like you're going to have to find some other babies to win your awards for you."

The judge brought a fist down hard on the table. "I want a paternity test."

"And you'll get one," Honey said, but her smile testified to how little the results worried her now.

Josie slipped the clean diaper under Troy, and Reed covered him up and fastened the tapes before they had a waterworks show all over the fancy law firm's conference room.

Honey gathered her son from the bench and plunked

him into Jimmy's arms, then took Emmie from Sam. The babies cooed in tandem as their mother and father cuddled them close and the four of them became a family.

Chapter Twenty

Tension enveloped Sam and John on the flight back from Dallas. John drove her to her house once again, the strained silence between them almost deafening. They hadn't spent any private time together since they'd found Honey. No dinners or phone calls.

No kisses or lovemaking.

Sam clenched her purse strap as he walked her to her door. She was so happy for Honey she wanted to cry. Honey had been searching for love all her life and now she'd found a good man who loved her, a man who'd fathered her twins and wanted to raise them with her.

Still she missed Honey already, and she missed those babies. She felt empty without them.

Her house seemed cold and so quiet it hurt as she unlocked the door. It was hard to believe it had only been a week since Honey had left Emmie in her house. But during that week, she'd realized she wanted love, too, a love like her best friend had found with Jimmy. And she wanted babies. Lots of them.

And she wanted them with John.

But his silence told her everything. He didn't want her. Their lovemaking had been a…convenience.

They'd been thrust together in a hotel room, in danger, and adrenaline and timing had brought them together. Now that that was over, there was no reason for them to see each other.

Except that she loved him fiercely.

So much that she had to let him go so he could pursue his dreams.

"Sam?" John said gruffly.

She turned to him, and memorized his face in the waning sunlight. "Yes."

"Will you be all right?"

His concern touched something deep inside her. He was a good man and deserved everything he wanted. So she lifted her chin. "Of course, John. You know me, I'm tough."

He studied her for a long moment, then lifted his hand and touched her cheek. A sad smile graced his eyes, then he leaned over and kissed her cheek. "Take care. And if you ever need anything…"

"I won't," she said, her throat thick. She had to go inside, get away from him before she broke down. So she turned and hurried inside, then shut the door between them.

Tears blurred her eyes as she leaned against the wall. She'd told him she was tough and she always had been.

So why was she falling apart at the thought of not seeing him again?

JOHN LET HIMSELF INSIDE his house, his head aching. He should be happy. He'd just solved a big case. Sam, Honey and Honey's children were safe. He'd finally received recognition for real police work, not rescuing those damned Butterbean dolls.

His phone trilled, and he checked the number. His father.

He grabbed the handset. "Hello, Dad."

"John, I called to congratulate you. Everyone is talking about you going up against Judge Theodore Wexler. It seems you made a name with that case after all."

Perspiration trickled down the side of John's jaw. "The most important thing is that Honey Dawson and her twins are safe, Dad."

"Well, of course. But you were brilliant. I want you to come to Atlanta next week. There's talk about a bid for the governor's office and your name came up."

John paced through his house, the quiet oppressive. This was his chance to leave town and be somebody. To finally please his father.

But Sam's face taunted him. Images of Sam fighting to save innocent children in need around the mountains. Sam standing up to monsters like Leonard Cultrain. Sam defending her friend Honey.

Of Sam kissing him. Sam making love to him.

Sam holding those babies.

His old insecurities rose to the surface, the memory of his high school girlfriend trying to trap him into marriage, then lying to him about her baby. Did Sam simply want a father for her own child?

Or could she possibly love him?

The tender way she'd touched him that night taunted him. The way she'd kissed him and given herself to him without asking for anything in return. The way she'd looked at him when they'd stood on her doorstep earlier.

Kind, caring, wonderful Sam wouldn't ask for anything.

And that made him love her even more.

Besides, Leonard Cultrain was still loose in town. And Sam would never give up her job. Dammit, she needed someone to take care of *her*.

And he wanted to be that somebody.

"John, I need your answer." His father's voice intruded into his thoughts. "I have to set things up right away."

John reached for his keys. "Dad, sorry, but I like my job here."

"What?"

"I said I'm staying."

"But you can't—"

"I can and I am," he said matter-of-factly. "And not only am I staying, but I'm going to investigate those accusations against Samantha Corley's father and prove his innocence."

"What? Have you gone mad?"

"Yes," he said. Madly in love. And he'd start the investigation right after he asked Sam to marry him.

SAM HAD CHANGED INTO her nightgown, but a noise suddenly startled her. Good heavens, who was out there now? Honey was safe. Teddy had admitted he'd shot at them in Dallas and was in jail. Sally had calmed down.

Leonard?

She flipped off the lights, grabbed her shotgun and raced down the stairs, then hid behind the door. A car engine died, and she peered out the side window, but it was so dark, she couldn't see what kind of vehicle it was. She braced the shotgun against her hip, just as a loud knock sounded on the door.

"Sam? It's me, John."

Her breath whooshed out, and she hurriedly unlatched the door.

John took one look at the shotgun and froze. "Sam, don't shoot."

She shivered, then laughed softly. "Sorry, I thought I heard a noise."

"You did. It was me."

She licked her lips, her chest still heaving, and suddenly realized she was wearing only a thin satin gown. She hadn't bothered to don a robe. His gaze raked over her, and he arched a brow, then reached up, took the gun and set it aside.

"What are you doing here?" Sam asked. "Is something wrong?"

"Yes," he said gruffly.

Her breath caught. "What? Is it Honey? The babies? Another child somewhere?"

He chuckled. "No, it's me."

She narrowed her eyes. "I don't understand."

"I thought I could let you go, Sam. That I could leave town, but I realized I can't."

A seed of hope sprouted inside her as his look darkened. "Why not, John?"

He pulled her to him and cradled her hips with his hands, then pressed his hard length against her. "Because I'm in love with you."

Her heart swelled with love and longing and desire. "You're in love with me?"

He nodded, then pressed a kiss to her cheek and neck. "Yeah. Wholeheartedly."

His sexy smile sent an erotic tingling through her. "I love you, too, John."

"Then you'll let me take care of you," he murmured against her neck.

She threaded her fingers into his hair. "I can take care of myself."

"Sam?"

She laughed and teased his lips apart with her tongue. "How about we take care of each other?"

"I like that plan," he said in a gruff voice, then slowly slid one strap of her gown off her shoulder. "I say we get started right now."

A sexy chuckle escaped him as he scooped her in his arms, carried her up the steps to her bedroom and stripped her.

Any joking turned to white-hot passion as they joined their bodies and hearts and made love until dawn. And when the sun cracked the sky, they snuggled together and vowed never to close the door between them again.

* * * * *

To hear what happened to baby Troy before he was reunited with Honey, be sure to pick up
COVERT COOTCHIE-COOTCHIE-COO
by Ann Voss Peterson, on sale now
from Harlequin Intrigue!

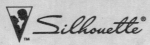

Silhouette®

Romantic
SUSPENSE

Sparked by Danger, Fueled by Passion.

The Agent's Secret Baby

by *USA TODAY* bestselling author
Marie Ferrarella

TOP SECRET DELIVERIES

Dr. Eve Walters suddenly finds herself pregnant
after a regrettable one-night stand and turns to an
online chat room for support. She eventually learns
the true identity of her one-night stand: a DEA agent
with a deadly secret. Adam Serrano does not want
this baby or a relationship, but can fear for Eve's
and the baby's lives convince him that this is what
he has been searching for after all?

Available October wherever books are sold.

**Look for upcoming titles in
the TOP SECRET DELIVERIES miniseries**

The Cowboy's Secret Twins by Carla Cassidy—November
The Soldier's Secret Daughter by Cindy Dees—December

Visit Silhouette Books at www.eHarlequin.com

SRS27650